DOCT

When Adele Kinsey is widowed and left to bring up
her four-year-old son on her own life seems bleak
indeed. So how can she bring herself to follow the
doctor's decree and learn to love again?

DOCTOR'S DECREE

BY
HELEN UPSHALL

MILLS & BOON LIMITED
London · Sydney · Toronto

First published in Great Britain 1982
by Mills & Boon Limited, 15–16 Brook's Mews,
London W1A 1DR

© Helen Upshall 1982

Australian copyright 1982
Philippine copyright 1982

ISBN 0 263 73864 7

03/0582/

Set in 10 on 10½ pt Linotron Times

Photoset by Rowland Phototypesetting Ltd
Bury St Edmunds, Suffolk
Made and printed in Great Britain by
Richard Clay (The Chaucer Press) Ltd
Bungay, Suffolk

My thanks to the directors of the Corinthian Health Club in Bournemouth for making our visit to the Unicorn Medical Screening Clinic in Birmingham possible, and to the medical staff there a special thank you for providing me with the background material for this novel.

CHAPTER ONE

'OLIVER. *Oliver!*'

Adele Kinsey gritted her teeth and then let out an impatient sigh. 'You naughty boy, Oliver. You know Mummy's in a hurry this morning. Now be quick and get dressed.'

It wasn't supposed to be 'one of those' mornings, Adele reflected, her white, china-like cheeks flushed to a deep pink. She cast a last glance at herself in the dressing-table mirror before going into the room next door where she found Oliver with his face buried in the bedspread.

'Darling,' she pleaded, her voice croaking as she tried to turn him over. 'Help Mummy—please?'

'Don't want to go,' he said flatly with a pronounced hiccup.

'Listen, Oliver. I'm sorry I shouted. It's just that—well— it's hard for Mummy too, you know. I have to start a new job, just like you're going to start at nursery school. We'll both have to be extra brave, so how about trying to help one another—eh?'

Oliver turned over on the bed, threw his arms round Adele and cried as if his heart would break.

If he only knew, Adele thought, how my heart aches too. Her eyes burned uncomfortably, but she simply must not cry. Not today; this was a new beginning as Matthew had said, and tears must be a thing of the past. But how could she not cry, when her four-year-old son was being pushed out to nursery school so that she could work? She didn't need to work she told herself for the hundredth time. She'd give in, go and telephone Matthew and explain. Hadn't Oliver been through enough already? Hadn't *she* suffered enough anguish without going through this unnecessary persecution?

It was no good appealing to Matthew though. This was all

his idea, and if she backed out now she'd be letting him down. If she really were going to chicken out she must ring the clinic and tell her new employer, Dr Gavin Forbes. Somehow the thought of showing him how weak she was made her pull herself together.

'Now, come along, Oliver,' she said brightly. 'There simply isn't time for any more cuddles this morning—where's that other sock?'

Was that really her voice? Firm and commanding? Oliver suddenly laughed.

'I can see it—under the chair,' he said pulling away from Adele's shoulder, and looking into her face.

'Then put it on quickly.'

With her heartstrings taut to breaking point she stood by patiently and waited while Oliver retrieved the lost sock. Her fingers itched to help him, but she could hear Matthew's reproachful voice.

'You're making a baby of him, Adele, and it will not do. All the mothering in the world won't make up for the loss of his father. I know it's hard, my dear, but you're on your own now and you've got to make a man of Oliver.'

A man—at four years old! God, how she'd wept—for Oliver, for herself, for Bernie.

How would she have coped without Matthew? Dear kind Matthew. Even in her nursing days she had known that the hospital's beloved Consultant, Dr Matthew Tyrell, seemed to have been endowed with more than the average share of compassionate understanding, but she had never imagined that he would take her under his wing so sympathetically. He had been a tower of strength all through Bernie's illness. An illness which unbeknown to Adele or her young husband had been eating away at his vitality undetected. When he had finally given way to it he had only six months left to fight, and they had both fought together for Oliver's sake, yet knowing in their innermost souls that it was a losing battle.

Adele allowed her mind to take a flight-path back to seven years ago when she had been nursing on the Women's Surgical Ward. A young, newly-qualified Staff

Nurse of twenty-two, caring for Bernie's mother who subsequently died from interminable cancer. She had warmed to Bernie in his grief. A young man of only twenty-five left to cope alone, but pity in her soft heart along with professional condolence had drawn her towards him and within a few short months they fell in love and married.

Bernie had cherished the new love he had to work for, and Adele's influence had encouraged him to rise to undreamed of heights in his work as an architect. They had scaled those heights together, realising so many of their dreams in a very short time, only to be awakened to that awful truth of Bernie's illness and the final parting.

Adele was grateful that Bernie had been a good businessman. She and Oliver were well provided for financially, but nothing could ever make up for the loss of the man she loved.

She blinked away the tears as in Oliver she saw Bernie. Dark, unruly hair, a wide, sudden smile which could capture any heart within seconds.

Adele turned away so that Oliver shouldn't see the moistness in her eyes.

'I just hope there won't be too much traffic, Oliver,' she said briskly, trying to appeal to his grown-up status.

She looked at her watch, realising that she had intended to leave at least ten minutes ago.

The traffic was heavy and when they eventually reached the nursery school Oliver became convulsed in sobs again.

'You won't go away and not come back like Daddy did, will you—promise, Mummy, promise?' he pleaded tearfully.

It took all her courage to be firm, but she knew Matthew was right. The stand had to be made. Oliver had to learn to trust her. She had to learn to make him independent.

The woman in charge of the nursery school took over with kind but firm reassurance, and Adele returned to the car unhappy, and angry with herself for not being able to control the tears which blurred her vision.

She listened; was it Oliver screaming? For a wild frantic moment she almost ran back to claim him and take him home, but in the car mirror she saw a young woman half dragging a distraught child towards the school gates.

Oliver might be unhappy at first, but he wouldn't be alone, and somehow this thought comforted Adele.

She started up the engine of her car and as she neared the city centre was aware of her own pounding heartbeats. She was going into the unknown alone. Someone would always turn up to protect Oliver, she could be pretty sure of that, but how was she going to fare?

Somewhere she heard a clock striking nine. That meant that she was late already, but as luck would have it she found a place easily in the car park, bought her ticket and then ran through the subway and up to the main shopping area.

No matter how much she hurried along she didn't feel she was making much headway, but at last she pushed open the huge glass doors, and inside checked that the *A Votre Santé* clinic was on the first floor as she remembered. 'To your good health,' she thought drily in translation.

The lift slid to a halt and the doors divided. Adele stepped out into immediate plush luxury. This was a far cry from hospital life and routine. No hustle and bustle here, not even any illness. Or that was what they hoped. This was the place where most people's niggling fears were assuaged; prevention better than cure being the motto.

An attractive receptionist was speaking softly into the telephone at the leather-padded corner desk. Adele approached cautiously, and as soon as the girl had finished her conversation she replaced the receiver and stood up.

'Mrs Kinsey, isn't it?' she asked with a smile.

'That's right and I'm afraid . . .'

'Dr Forbes was just asking if you'd arrived. Will you come this way.'

Adele's feet sank into the deep pile carpet as she followed the receptionist noiselessly through a passageway to a teak-veneered door.

DOCTOR GAVIN FORBES the name-plate read, and Adele felt her stomach heave. There was no reason to feel so nervous. At her interview she had met this man—a friend of Matthew's—who had been polite, but not, she recalled, particularly friendly, but then he wouldn't be, she supposed. His interest was purely professional.

He remained sitting at his desk as she offered a humble 'Good morning', and the receptionist left the office, closing the door softly.

'Good morning, Mrs Kinsey. Not a very good time-keeper perhaps?' His slow drawl broke the silence.

Adele's shadowed eyes met his appraising ones across the desk. He looked quite fierce for what one would normally describe as a good-looking man. His hair was a dark straw colour with auburn tints in it and his eyebrows were fair and thick. His lips were pressed together, finely chiselled lips, which, no doubt, hid a certain terseness of manner.

The reference to her bad time-keeping caught her unprepared. She hadn't expected a reproach on her first day. She had Oliver to think about. Was he still crying? Did he hate her for going off and leaving him with strangers? She felt all the fullness of her emotions swell within her breast, and as she opened her mouth to explain, all that would materialise was a cry of anguish. All that she had striven to keep inside, to bottle up, came gushing forth in a deluge of uncontrollable weeping.

'Please sit down, Mrs Kinsey.'

Dr Gavin Forbes spoke quietly, and then, clicking a button on the intercom on his desk, said: 'Bring two cups of tea, Katy,' with a hint of patient forbearance.

Adele fumbled with a tissue; this was unforgivable, she seemed unable to restrain her emotion.

She walked to the huge curtained picture window and hid her face, but after some attention to it while making sure she kept her back to her new employer, she turned and spoke in a trembling voice.

'I'm—terribly—sorry.' She paused for fear of a fresh outburst. 'I . . . I didn't like leaving my little boy.'

Dr Gavin Forbes kept his head bent over his paperwork, as if he hadn't even heard her speak. He continued to write until the receptionist arrived with a tray bearing two cups of

tea. Then he merely glanced up quite unconcerned as he
waved a hand towards an easy chair at one corner of the
desk.

'Do sit down, please, Mrs Kinsey,' he repeated.

She accepted the tea gratefully, but hated the man
behind the desk for his lack of sympathy. She detected a
hint of sarcasm in his tone, and she felt sure he was laughing
inwardly at her distress.

After what seemed like several minutes he put down the
long gold pen and sat back in his chair, clasping his two
hands across his waist.

'Oliver, isn't it? Matthew tells me a robust, healthy
young man—hopefully like Dickens' Oliver—always
asking for more.'

Adele glanced up in time to see a tantalising smile flicker
across Dr Forbes's face.

'I appreciate that this is quite an ordeal—though more
for his Mum, I suspect,' he continued gently.

Adele wanted to explode with all her fears, in defence of
Oliver too, but she felt ill-at-ease. This man was amused by
the whole scene. He had no feelings, obviously no children,
she thought aggressively. She felt the urge to run. This was
all a ghastly mistake, she had known it from the start.
Matthew for once was wrong. He might be a clever consultant in his own field, but he didn't know anything about
heartache, or children and their problems. She should
never have listened to him.

She looked up again at the man behind the desk. His eyes
were clearer now, green, flecked with some indeterminate
colour, and his hair wasn't like straw at all but burnished
gold. His complexion was fresh, his face a distinct square
shape with a pronounced dimple in each cheek. He didn't
speak and neither could Adele. She accepted his scrutiny of
her for as long as she dared and then with colour suffusing
her cheeks she looked away.

'Our girls like to be known by their Christian names.
Adele, isn't it? So, drink your tea, Adele,' he advised
kindly.

She sipped obediently. It did calm her nerves.

'By now young Oliver has made friends and is playing happily. Nature has a remarkable way of helping children through a crisis. That doesn't mean that I'm not sympathetic to your feelings though, Adele.'

Adele managed to meet his gaze boldly as she said tongue in cheek: 'You're very kind, and patient. I think perhaps I was wrong, after all. I should have waited until Oliver reaches the proper school age—a little more time—we could have had a little more time together.'

Gavin Forbes studied Adele closely for a moment then his glance fell to the paperwork on his desk.

'Time does help, of course. How long is it since your husband died, Adele?'

Adele fingered the handle of the cup nervously. How could he be so cruel? To talk about Bernie so coldly, so indifferently.

'Four months,' she said quietly.

'That sounds a reasonable time to me. Picking up the pieces is never easy, be it four months or four years. Would you really be helping Oliver to possess and protect him? You'd still have the first day of school to overcome eventually.'

'But you see I don't need to work,' she explained hurriedly. 'It seems selfish. Matthew thought . . .' She hesitated. Matthew was a friend of Dr Forbes and she had resolved that she wouldn't use him. He had spoken for her to get this job, not because she wanted it, but because Matthew thought it best for her and Oliver.

'Matthew considered that *you* needed something to occupy your mind, Adele,' Gavin Forbes reminded her gently.

'But I have Oliver. Children are a full-time job.'

'You're a fully-qualified nursing sister, Adele. You're intelligent, young and capable, and need to be stretched.'

A solemn silence fell between them. She had heard these same words, or similar, from Matthew, but in her lonely wakeful hours of darkness she wanted only to love and protect Oliver, even though in more rational moments she believed Matthew to be right.

Gavin Forbes stood up.

'Put your energies in to the new routine, Adele,' he counselled, walking round the desk and propping himself up against it. 'Give Oliver a break, a chance to grow and express himself. As for yourself—well—we'll do our best to keep you busy and not allow you time to indulge in self-pity.'

Adele placed the cup and saucer on his desk and stood up.

'I'm sure I've wasted too much of your time already. I'll give it a try, but I just don't think it will work. I'm grateful to you anyway for giving me the opportunity.'

'Sometimes in life, Adele, we *have* to make things work. I don't employ my nurses to "give it a try". We're here to give time to our patients, time and all our attention to their problems and worries, and I shall expect no less a standard from you. In fact, in the circumstances I shall expect more consideration.'

Adele felt herself expand with indignation. He should practise what he preaches she thought, and was irritated when he put a comforting arm round her shoulder.

'Let's go and introduce you to some of the girls who will show you the ropes. It is, as I told you when we met ten days ago, much more relaxed than hospital nursing. Much less demanding in terms of caring for a number of sick people at one time. Here the patient has the undivided attention of a doctor for an hour-long consultation, and the nurse or radiographer for the tests for as long as it takes.'

At the door he paused, and it seemed to Adele that he took a maddeningly long time to remove his hand from her shoulder, allowing it to soothe her back gently and come to rest at her waist. She glanced across to meet his hard green eyes. He raised an eyebrow and inclined his head to one side with a smile which suddenly turned his eyes to a sparkling turquoise shade, and as his lips parted generously they revealed pearly-white even teeth.

'We shan't let you do anything too exacting today, Adele,' he explained, 'but I want you to know that my door is always open, be your problems personal or in connection with the clinic.'

She murmured her gratitude.

'If you give us a chance, Adele, I'm sure we can help you as well as benefitting from having a charming new nursing sister as part of our team.'

Adele found herself looking at the door handle as if begging him to allow her to leave. She remembered how strong she had intended to show him she was, instead she had made a fool of herself, and now he was placating her.

He opened the door and she walked by his side through some double doors to a large waiting area.

Huge windows afforded a view over the large Midlands city, and plush seats in a warm orange colour were set in one corner round a low magazine table. This arrangement was repeated in the opposite corner, and at the other end of the long window there were cupboards, a desk, and coffee-making equipment.

Two girls were at the desk in earnest conversation, but stopped as Dr Forbes and Adele approached. He introduced her to them: 'This is Sheila, our senior sister, the only full-time one, and Denise.' He glanced from them to Adele and back again to the senior sister. 'Sheila, I'll leave Adele in your capable hands. Show her around and see her through all the necessary tests so that she is completely familiar with them before she has a patient to herself.' He turned to go, then changed his mind and faced Adele again. 'Perhaps being your first day we'll make a small concession—Sheila, I suggest that Adele leaves half an hour or so early in order to reach nursery school in good time to pick up her young son. By this evening, my dear, you'll be wondering what all the fuss was about.'

He smiled, the kind of smile which Adele found patronising, and watching him walk across the springy Axminster carpet she briefly wondered how on earth such a man could be a friend of Matthew's.

It did not take Adele long to discover that her appointment had been viewed with reservations. Her colleagues were aware that she had been introduced to Dr Gavin

Forbes by Dr Matthew Tyrell, and that her circumstances were such that she must be shown sympathy and understanding.

Adele did her best to be pleasant and interested in her work, trying to hide the fear, and deeper feelings which simmered so close to the surface. She was fitted out with a smart new uniform which consisted of a pleated skirt in a pretty shade of green, flecked with white. Under the collar of a white cotton shirt she wore a green and white patterned silk scarf which bore the name of the clinic. When actually taking a patient round on the various tests she was required to wear a short white overall piped with green and at all times wore a neat enamel brooch bearing her name.

As the first morning passed incredibly quickly Adele became absorbed in the running of the private medical screening clinic. Denise was one of the qualified radiographers who carried out chest X-rays, and mammograph X-rays on women patients. The rest of the team of eight qualified nurses took patients, both men and women, through hearing and sight, lung-function and ECG tests as well as exercise-tolerance measurement and recording the patient's height and weight measurements. Each test was carried out in individual rooms where the utmost privacy was observed. The hour-long consultation between patient and doctor was in a larger, more plush consulting room, where a nurse was in attendance only while the doctor carried out a cervical smear test on women patients as well as breast and pelvic examination. Blood tests, a vital part of the screening routine, were taken by a doctor, and haematological and biochemical profiles sent to London for analysis. All this was done in an atmosphere of friendly liaison, the emphasis being on ensuring that the patient was relaxed throughout the two-hour-long screening session. Adele was much impressed by all that she learned, realising the value of such a clinic, and wondering if Bernie had attended a clinic for such a check-up would he have had his illness diagnosed in time for treatment to be effective? . . .

*   *   *

When Adele drove out of the car park later she was convinced that Matthew had been right after all, but for the wrong reasons. Of course Oliver had to learn to be independent, and she must school herself against becoming over-possessive, but most of all to be doing a worthwhile job, helping any unfortunate victims of heart disease or cancer to be aware of their problems so that they could act upon the advice passed on to their own general practitioners was all in a good cause, and in memory of her darling Bernie for whom life had ended so early. She reproached herself for her tears and anguish earlier, and resolved that she must rearrange her life in accordance with her new job. It wouldn't be easy. Just four months without Bernie had shown her how much she had relied on her husband and now with no family in the immediate neighbourhood she was forced to come to terms with the fact that she and Oliver were a one-parent family. It was a comfort to know that Matthew was always on hand should she need advice. Her own parents had emigrated to Canada, so Matthew had filled her need of a father-figure, and in some ways was filling the same need for Oliver since Bernie's death.

Just one morning doing something positive had given Adele an uplift; something else besides Oliver to care about and work for.

Matthew sometimes helped out at the clinic. He had been a friend of Gavin Forbes for some time so Adele knew that her new boss was going to revel in telling Matthew about her distress that morning. They would expect her to be ready to give in, especially if Oliver was unhappy at nursery school. She pulled up outside the hall and sat waiting. Despite Dr Forbes' suggestion that she should leave early she had been too engrossed in the routine at the clinic to avail herself of his offer, and had left only ten minutes before one o'clock. Her fingers idly tapped on the steering wheel in an attempt to will away her agitation. She was desperately longing to see Oliver, but common sense told her that if she started appearing before the rest of the Mums Oliver would expect it every day. It was an agonising suspense, but she was able to watch other girls coming to

wait for their small children. She recognised the young
woman who had been forced to leave her screaming child.
She appeared well-dressed and self-confident and seemingly unperturbed. Adele pursed her lips, remembering her
own image in the mirror. Six months ago Bernie had called
her 'Pudding', but in so short a time her radiant cheeks had
lost their glow and her clothes hung loosely over what
seemed a skeleton of her former self. Matthew assured her
that in time she would pick up, that she would find things to
smile about again—she must, he so often warned—for
Oliver's sake.

Two or three children came skipping up to the gate with
shouts of glee at freedom, smiling, eager expressions searching for the familiar face that meant so much to them.

Some mothers began to crowd around the door as a
helper appeared looking for certain Mums. Adele remained where she was, clenching her fists tightly in self-
control until several children had gone, and then she
walked sedately up the path to the hall door.

Mrs Dawkins greeted her with a warm smile. Adele was
grateful that as a semi-retired teacher Mrs Dawkins was a
middle-aged homely, motherly sort of woman.

'Can't pull him away from his building,' Mrs Dawkins
said cheerfully, then placing a comforting hand on Adele's
arm she added: 'Come along in, Mrs Kinsey, and admire his
handiwork. He's been fine, honestly. A little withdrawn
perhaps, not very much to say, but that's only to be
expected on the first morning. We'll give him a fortnight,
then pass him on to our young nursery teacher for an
assessment.' She walked through the corridor with Adele,
explaining again the general routine of the private nursery
school. 'Jean Abbot is well-qualified and she's married with
two of her own so she knows how to manage them.'

At the door to the main room they paused and Adele
watched as Oliver, with solemn expression, fitted another
small coloured brick into place.

'An architect in the making I shouldn't wonder,' Mrs
Dawkins said with a laugh.

'That wouldn't be surprising,' Adele agreed. 'His father

was an architect and had Oliver building before he could walk almost.'

Adele recalled with nostalgia the two dark heads close together, diligently working until the new hotel or high-rise flats, on occasion the Spanish villa which was Bernie's prize ambition, had been completed, only to be demolished in a flash by a boisterous Oliver, much to Bernie's disgust.

'I'll leave him to you,' Mrs Dawkins suggested. 'You must be prepared for some out-of-character behaviour during this first couple of weeks.' She glanced at Adele intently. 'How was *your* first day?'

Adele hesitated, not wanting to remember her arrival at the clinic.

'Interesting,' she said apprehensively. 'I suppose I shall eventually get used to all the changes.'

'Change is as good as a rest, they say, m'dear, and you're young, you'll cope—come along, young Oliver, Mummy's here.'

Oliver put down the brick in his hand as if it were red hot, and Adele felt a pang of commiseration. Had he learnt total obedience in so short a time? And at what cost? Adele was consumed with regrets all over again. He wasn't going to be hers any more. Other people were going to have a hand in his upbringing—all his endearing little ways would be spoilt now as he learnt how to survive among the other children.

'Hullo, darling,' Adele said as Oliver glanced eagerly from Mrs Dawkins to her. Then he smiled that sudden, special smile which instantly reminded her of Bernie, and with a whoop of delight flung himself at Adele.

'We'll leave your building just as it is, Oliver, then you can finish it tomorrow,' Mrs Dawkins assured him.

Oliver stood back from Adele and looked up at the ample form of Mrs Dawkins. He didn't smile but stared at the older woman as if not quite sure how to react to her authority.

'That will be nice, won't it, Oliver?' Adele prompted, and as she took his hand and led him away, she exchanged a knowing nod with the older woman.

Oliver scrambled into the back seat of the car and Adele

secured her safety belt. Before starting up the engine she took a glance in the mirror at Oliver who had shrunk into the corner and seemed to be examining his shoes.

'What else have you done besides building?' she asked, looking over her shoulder.

'Nothing,' came the plaintive reply, and Adele experienced a shiver of cold fear for him.

All the way home Oliver remained still and silent in his corner, and as they pulled up in the driveway of the smart four-bedroomed detached house, elegantly designed by Bernie, Adele said in a high-pitched, over-joyful voice: 'Here we are then—home again,' to try to bring him back to life, but still he remained untalkative.

Adele didn't feel much like talking herself, but she wanted Oliver to be his normal exuberant self, yet she recognised his need of readjustment, and so she went straight to the kitchen to prepare lunch. Tomato soup, she decided, that was his favourite, followed by scrambled egg on toast, and then a rest watching television while she did a few jobs. She had to do some reorganising too. Since Bernie's death she well might have become a recluse if it hadn't been for Oliver. Even then she had kept 'going out' to the minimum. Bernie had died in spring, so she and Oliver had spent any hot summery days that came along in the large garden, swimming in Bernie's luxurious swimming pool, not feeling the need to go out except to shop, and that for just the two of them was only necessary once a month by kind permission of her large well-stocked freezer. Now suddenly they had both been pushed into the big outside world. As she stood stirring the thick red liquid Adele was surprised to realise how much she had enjoyed her morning at the clinic which had provided a new interest on which to centre her thoughts.

When she went to call Oliver to come to the dining room she found him in the huge square hall lying on the colourful oval rug.

'Lunch is ready, Oliver,' she called from the doorway watching as he rolled from side to side. He didn't appear to have heard her so she went and knelt by his side.

'You're home now, darling,' she whispered softly. 'Come and see—I've prepared your favourite.'

His large dark eyes settled on Adele's face, and slowly focussed as if seeing her for the first time. She helped him to his feet and he went passively with her to the dining room.

Adele's heart ached with love for him. What was she doing to her child? How could she face the future, the long adventurous years of his growing up, alone, without Bernie?

Half way through his soup he looked up suddenly and smiled endearingly.

'Did you like it at Uncle Matthew's clinic?' he asked.

Adele choked back the tears and managed to smile. She nodded.

'Yes—yes, I did like it, darling. Everyone was very nice to me.' She took another spoonful of soup. 'And how did you like it at nursery school?'

He gave a big exhausted sigh and propped his elbow on the table, resting his cheek on his hand.

'It was all right. There was a naughty boy there—he kicked Mrs Dawkins.'

Adele looked shocked. 'That was awful.'

Oliver finished the remainder of his lunch in silence and Adele appreciated that he needed to think deeply about this new way of life.

They ate as usual around six, and when Adele had washed up and cleared away she helped Oliver prepare for bed, and then they sat on the settee together for his nightly story. She knew that he might not sleep instantly as he had slept after lunch so she read for a little longer than usual. Oliver was a bright little boy who loved listening while Adele read, often stopping her to ask questions or converse quite intelligently for a four year old. Adele wanted her son to regard her as his friend, a good companion, as well as his mother, and she resolved that whatever tasks she had to do, this hour before bedtime must always be Oliver's.

She was rather crestfallen when the story was interrupted by a peal of the front door chimes.

'Oh, finish the story,' Oliver pleaded.

'I must answer the door,' she said getting to her feet slowly from the cramped position she had got into on the settee.

Through the leafy design of the glass front door she knew before she opened it that it was Matthew.

'Hullo, my dear,' he greeted happily. 'Thought I'd come early. I expect young Oliver's tired out after his first day at school.'

Adele stood aside to let Matthew pass then closed the door, sensing within herself a strange indignation at his intrusion.

CHAPTER TWO

'Not in bed yet, young man?' Matthew greeted as he followed Adele into the lounge.

'He slept after lunch so we're having an extra long read this evening,' Adele explained. 'Would you like the rest of the story here or in bed, darling?' she asked Oliver.

'In bed,' he whispered softly and took Adele's hand eagerly.

'Uncle Matthew won't mind not being entertained for a few minutes. I know it's rather rude,' Adele apologised, glancing briefly at Matthew, 'but just for once—we'd reached the exciting part, hadn't we, Oliver? Do help yourself to a drink, Matthew, I'll be down in a few moments.'

Matthew held up a hand. 'Don't hurry it on my account,' he said agreeably. 'No piggy-back tonight, Oliver?'

Oliver tightened his grasp on Adele's hand and sucking his cheeks in anxiously shook his head.

'Goodnight then—God bless,' Matthew said in his usual pleasant way.

Adele felt a trifle guilty that Matthew was without company, but surely a doctor would understand, she thought as she sat on the edge of Oliver's divan and continued until the last two pages had been read. She didn't hurry away, giving Oliver the opportunity to talk if he wanted to, but he put his chubby hands around her neck and hugged her until at last she broke free.

'Now off to sleep quickly, darling, we mustn't be late again tomorrow.'

'Did you get into trouble?' Oliver asked, wide-eyed.

'No—but it was a bad way to begin a new job, and it's not a good habit, always having to rush.'

She kissed him again and then left him, briefly going into the large room she had shared with Bernie, combing her

23

hair and touching up her make-up before returning to the lounge where she found Matthew relaxing comfortably in one of the recliner chairs. He hadn't heard her coming, but when she closed the door he stood up.

'Can I get you something?' he asked, indicating with his own glass.

'No, thanks. I'm sorry, Matthew—' but he cut her short by saying:

'I don't like drinking alone, and as you know, Adele, I'm a great believer in a small sherry for a daily tonic.'

He went across to the far wall where shelves contained books on one side, a lavish music centre and hi-fi equipment on the other with a small but well-stocked drinks cabinet in the centre.

Adele had been irritated by his arrival, but now she studied the back of Matthew Tyrell. He was very tall, lanky would be an apt description, with long arms which at times she suspected he didn't quite know how to manage. The dark blue suit he was wearing was expensive and well-cut, designed to hide his slightly bent back. A thin patch of hair was visible on the back of his head, hair that had been black but now with its grey streaks was a sign of his forty-five years. He was still good-looking, especially when he smiled as he did now, turning, holding a sherry schooner between slender fingers. He had a long face with a straight nose, a high and wide forehead, part of which was hidden by the soft fall of a wave of his dark hair. The upper rim of his spectacles was gold, the rest part rimless which added a certain distinguished elegance to his appearance. Adele smiled in return, acknowledging how much gratitude she owed to Matthew.

When her parents had flown over to be with her at the time of Bernie's death, Matthew had promised that he would always be on hand to guide her, that he would never let her down, and he had kept his promise. Guilt at her earlier resentment caused her cheeks to flush as she accepted the sherry from him. She dropped her gaze to the amber liquid.

'Has it been a day to remember?' he enquired.

The events of the day crowded her already confused brain. Tears of agitation were ever-ready to be shed, instead she looked up at Matthew defiantly.

'I'm sure your friend, Dr Forbes, gave you all the details—the pathetic, sordid details,' she said bitterly.

Matthew kept his gaze fixed firmly on her face. A face which he considered quite lovely whether carrying an expression of sweet humility, sad loneliness, or even now when for the very first time he saw the liquid dark brown eyes smarting with anger.

He didn't answer so that Adele, unable to meet his questioning stare turned and walked to the settee.

Matthew followed slowly and stood behind it.

'I haven't seen or spoken to Gavin,' he said, softly. 'I imagine the day has not been without its doubtful moments. If you want to talk, go ahead, I'm listening, but if you'd rather be alone, Adele, I shall quite understand.'

Adele couldn't answer, neither would the tears which so often were an excuse for non-communication materialise. She sipped her drink, and after what seemed an eternity she slowly, hesitantly, told Matthew all that had happened.

Matthew made no attempt to interrupt or even sit beside her. When she had explained everything he casually went to refill his empty glass, and then as non-committally returned to the recliner across the room.

'Gavin is a most understanding person, Adele,' he assured her. 'I'm sure he didn't intend to sound over-authoritative regarding your being late. He will appreciate that there are adjustments to be made, and I congratulate you on being sensible enough not to fetch Oliver early. This next two weeks will be difficult for you both, and you'll have to be extremely careful that you don't spoil Oliver.'

Adele grunted. 'You've already accused me of doing that,' she said despondently.

'No, my dear, I haven't. I've only warned you of the obvious dangers. You've been in an emotional state and children are quick to take advantage.'

'Oliver hasn't,' she argued hastily. 'He wouldn't—children of his age don't understand enough to take advantage.'

'Children are much more ingenious than we give them credit for. They are alert to atmosphere—quick to sense a parent's weakness.'

'I really can't see it working, Matthew. I should have waited. It's much too soon, for Oliver and me. You can't expect a man like Dr Forbes to appreciate my difficulties.'

'Now you're being absurd, Adele. Gavin is a doctor, and he wouldn't have reached consultant level if he weren't intelligent enough to understand his patients.'

'I didn't mean in a professional way,' Adele said splaying her hands in despair. 'I'm not a patient, for one thing.' She got up and walked round the room. 'I don't know his personal details, of course,' she conceded half-heartedly, 'but unless he's known private grief, how can he know what it's like?—and children—what does *he* know about children? Has he any of his own?'

She confronted Matthew almost aggressively.

Matthew raised his soft blue eyes to gaze at Adele's flushed cheeks.

'He isn't married, my dear.' He reached out and caught her hand, 'so he hasn't any family that I know of.' A smile hovered around his lips.

Suddenly Adele pulled her hand free, aware of the contact between herself and Matthew. She almost hurried to the bar and without realising it poured herself another sherry. It wasn't the first time there had been any physical contact between them. Matthew had been her support for so long now that she had come to regard him as—?

What was he to her? Such a dear, kind friend she acknowledged silently, and her thoughts flew back to her working days when she had admired his gentle manner, and the compassion he bestowed so generously upon his patients. First Bernie's mother and later Bernie himself. How soothing his touch had been she remembered as he had sat opposite her in a small room at the hospital and told her what she had already suspected, that Bernie's illness was interminable. He had answered all her questions with patience, but above all, honesty, for which she had been grateful, and during those timeless days when hope for Bernie, for Oliver, for herself seemed the only thing to live for they had grown together and become—friends? Of course that's all it is, she convinced herself, angry that more vagrant thoughts had intruded into their innocent relationship.

Matthew stood up abruptly and, with unusual brusqueness for him, said: 'I expect you have things to do. I understand your restlessness, Adele. Be patient, my dear, give yourself time to adapt.'

Adele looked up at him, afraid of the private knowledge of a pending new relationship with Matthew. Outwardly she had shown impatience but inwardly she was ready to turn to him for reassurance.

'I may see you at the clinic,' he said casually. 'I have a morning session there on Thursday morning. A heavy list at the hospital though on Friday and Saturday, but you know where I am if you need me.'

Adele placed the sherry schooner back on the drop-down glass bar-top.

'Matthew—I'm sorry if I sound ungrateful—I'm not— you know that. I guess I'm just a bit wound up. Having to work again—' she shrugged, 'takes some getting used to.'

'You must keep occupied, Adele,' he said sternly. 'You're young—live life to the full—isn't that what Bernie would have wanted?'

She nodded and tried to smile. 'I expect so.'

'I *know* so.' He squeezed her arm briefly. 'I shall be playing golf over at Latcham Green on Sunday morning, probably have lunch at the Club there, so I'll look in on Sunday evening.' He strode briskly to the door and across the square hall, his heels on the parquet flooring making a decisive clatter and then he was gone.

Adele stood and stared at the closed front door. Through the glass she saw the reflection as his car did a U-turn before gliding down the drive and away.

It was past nine o'clock and she hadn't offered him

coffee, but he usually stayed later and he had never left so abruptly before.

She went to the door, secured the lock and chain and then went to the kitchen. Being alone she decided on a malted milk drink rather than coffee, and as she switched on the television and sipped her drink she pondered over the change in Matthew's attitude. He hadn't said he would ring, but of course he would, he did most nights even when he was in London or Scotland and even once from Germany when he had been on holiday. She found she was unable to concentrate on the programme. Matthew's determined footsteps across the hall still echoed in her head, and between her and the characters on the screen dancing like mechanical puppets she could see Matthew's gentle gaze. Why was she suddenly analysing him, and everything he said or did? Because, she thought miserably, today everything has changed. Today was the start of a new life, no matter how much she wanted to cling to the old one. She knew that Matthew was right about that at least, she had to create a future for herself, but most of all for Oliver. It came to her then like a sledge-hammer crashing down on to a tree-trunk. Matthew was pulling out! He had kept his promise to her parents, helped her to get through the past four months and was now forcing her to stand on her own two feet. He could have given her a little more time surely, until she had come to terms with her job, with Oliver at nursery school. Beneath all his charm and generosity she supposed Matthew had become bored with his paternal role.

Adele felt her cheeks tighten before the blood rushed into them. Could Matthew have had other ideas? He was fifteen years her senior, a distinguished and much loved consultant with whom she had worked, and who, because of their professional relationship, had decreed that he should be her guardian in her hour of need.

He wasn't married. Somehow she had never given the matter a great deal of thought, but now she recalled how during her nursing days most of the spinster senior sisters at the hospital had at some time made a play for him, ever hopeful, but never successful in their quest.

The tender gleam in his blue eyes came back to taunt her, along with the touch of his hand holding hers. How stupid she had been, imagining that he had taken her under his wing out of sheer good-heartedness. How selfish *she* had been! Weeping on his shoulder, seeking his advice, encouraging him to take Bernie's place—No, not that, *never*—her heart cried out in anguish! No one could ever do that.

Adele drained her mug, realising just how defenceless she was at twenty-nine years of age. Of course men would quickly forget her heartache, and all that she had been through, and expect her to respond to their appeal. This thought made her angry, and she uncurled her slim legs from beneath her on the couch and went quickly to turn off the television.

In the kitchen she remained motionless at the sink, deep in thought. In her grief she had turned to Matthew, naive enough to believe that his compassion was genuine, that he was concerned for her and Oliver. It was horrible, almost degrading to think of him viewing her in any other way.

She stared vacantly into the darkness after she had peeped in to see that Oliver was sleeping peacefully. She was imagining things. Matthew was the same as he had always been, a father figure, ready to advise and be on hand when he was needed. He wouldn't desert her now, and neither did he expect anything from her. But the element of doubt had presented itself and would not be pushed away, so that Adele went on staring into the darkness until well after midnight. She was awake again by six and got up at once rather than oversleep. She didn't feel particularly rested but still hounded by confusion in trying to understand Matthew's change of attitude.

On reaching the clinic though, Matthew's influence faded into obscurity as her interest developed during the hours she spent accompanying her colleagues when they took clients through the various tests. She was surprised to find that even Oliver subsided into a corner of her mind. Meeting people, being forced to converse socially as well as the technical side of her new job helped her to come alive again and gave her a positive reason to emerge from her shadow of grief. Although not a qualified radiographer Adele found it interesting to watch Denise at work taking chest X-rays, and mammograms on women patients, and she soon learnt the routine as well as absorbed the main aims of *A Votre Santé* clinic, the need of clinical examination on well people, alleviating fears, and in some cases detecting disease in the early stages so that treatment could commence and hopefully a cure be effected.

Oliver's morning tears decreased, indicating that he too had become accustomed to the dramatic change in his young life, but Adele tried not to notice that with this change came a total lack of communication. Each day he seemed more reticent than the one before. Adele felt miserable, blaming herself for Oliver's distress, feeling almost guilty at the pleasure she personally gained from her work at the clinic. She wrestled with her conscience. She must refuse to be influenced by Matthew or Gavin Forbes, and sacrifice her own desires for Oliver.

Despite the fact that the verbal agreement made between herself and Dr Forbes had been a month's trial, a month's notice on either side, she convinced herself that she ought to make her apologies to her boss and offer him a week's notice. She suspected that he would be glad to get rid of her. Employers didn't like staff with personal problems, and, after all, he had only employed her to please Matthew. He might even let her leave on Friday. Deep down she knew she didn't want to give up so easily but her loyalties became confused the more she dwelt upon them.

Time passed incredibly quickly as she fell into the new routine a job created, and she was agreeably surprised two mornings later when Sheila handed her a clipboard.

'You're on your own from now on, Adele,' she said kindly. 'You could have been from the start actually, but you just needed a few days to get the general idea and gain some confidence. Just carry on as you did yesterday morning and you'll be fine.'

Adele smiled. 'I can always sing out if I get into any

difficulty,' she said. 'It seems so strange to have time to talk to my patients—'

'Clients,' Sheila corrected. 'We don't offer any treatment, we just hope we'll discover any cause for treatment even before any symptoms appear.'

'It's all very worthwhile. In hospital work you'd dearly love to be able to spare the time to chat, but with so much on your mind, and numerous other patients awaiting attention, it's just impossible.'

'Yes,' Sheila agreed. 'Dr Forbes is very adamant about being warm and friendly, and letting clients take their time. This is a good job for us married women as there aren't the pressures of hospital life.'

The intercom buzzed and after Sheila had listened briefly she turned to Adele.

'Mr and Mrs Edwards have arrived—good luck, Adele.'

Adele walked across the large lounge, everything so luxuriously comfortable, and much more like an hotel than a clinic which must ease, if only slightly, the apprehension which most clients experienced on their first visit. She passed through the swing doors, along a short passageway into the reception area where she found two couples, heads bent over an exotic plant in the stonework, hexangular-shaped ornamental garden. Katy, the receptionist, was there too, laughing as she said: 'This plant gets everyone going, but I couldn't even attempt to pronounce the name of it. It only survives because of the heat from the lighting and the constant flow of water supplied by the miniature fountain.' She turned. 'Are you any good at foreign plants, Adele?'

'Afraid not, Katy. My own garden holds sufficient mystery for me and causes enough headaches.'

'Then I should leave it all to your husband, my dear,' one of the men said.

Adele felt a cold shiver run down her spine, but she smiled in acknowledgement to the jovial gentleman. He wasn't to know about her private sorrow, and references to her marital state must be expected in her dealings with members of the public, so it was something she had to get used to.

Katy came to the rescue eagerly.

'Mr and Mrs Edwards, this is your nurse for today—Adele,' she introduced.

Shaking hands with the more senior of the two couples Adele invited them to follow her back to the lounge.

'You're new here, aren't you?' Mrs Edwards ventured.

Adele affirmed this with a wry smile. 'Very new,' she said. 'Evidently you've attended the clinic before?'

'This is our third visit,' Mr Edwards informed her enthusiastically. 'We came as soon as Dr Forbes opened the clinic. We're both extremely fit for our ages and that's how we mean to stay. General practitioners are always rushed off their feet. We like coming here, although I must admit it was a bit unnerving the first time when we didn't quite know what to expect. There's such a nice friendly atmosphere here and the doctor has time to listen. When the reports come through pronouncing us A1 it sets our minds at rest for another year.'

Adele took their coats, hanging them on hangers on the rail provided.

'You know the drill better than me I expect then,' she said cheerfully. 'Mr Edwards, if you'd go with Denise for your chest X-ray, I'll see you afterwards, and if you're ready, Mrs Edwards, we'll go along to Dr Forbes's consulting room.'

It was important not to hurry anyone, but Mrs Edwards, an attractive, youthful-looking fifty year old, seemed eager. She grinned knowingly at Adele.

'I'm ready for *him* any time,' she whispered confidentially, 'he's a lovely man.'

As they walked the length of a long, carpeted passageway, passing some of the smaller rooms where the various tests were carried out, Gavin Forbes appeared at the door at the end. He greeted his patient warmly. 'How nice to see you again, Mrs Edwards,' he said, showing a liberal helping of professional charm. Adele could see at a glance why clients would fall for him. Like the average doctor, well-groomed, handsome, not only in looks but by virtue of his profession, and of necessity a pleasant manner. Experience had taught Adele not to trust this surface show of courteous respect. Doctors in particular seemed to have split personalities, all except Matthew, and he was always the same. Already she had been the victim of Dr Gavin Forbes's sudden change of mood. The sarcasm behind the charm, the indifference to her distress on that first morning. He unnerved her, and in the following fleeting exchange of glances as he indicated that Adele could leave Mrs Edwards in his care, she knew that she simply wouldn't suit him as employee, she would never succeed in pleasing him. So far, during her first three days, she hadn't come into contact with the head of the clinic, but today he was in evidence and she being on her own as it were she supposed it was make or break day. Had she imagined it, or had there been a silent warning in that flicker of his eyes towards her?

She returned to the lounge, glad that for a while she could concentrate on Mr Edwards and his tests.

A few moments later her client emerged from the X-ray room with Denise. He was carrying his jacket and tie.

'Shall I take those?' Adele offered, but already Mr Edwards was making his own way to the coat-rail.

'I'll put my tie in my pocket and hang my jacket up out of the way. Clothes are just a nuisance,' he added with a saucy wink.

'They do get in the way rather on these occasions,' Adele agreed, and led the stocky middle-aged man to the first of the test rooms where Adele charted Mr Edwards's height and weight, comparing the latter with the predicted weight taking into account his build and age.

'Not much to worry about there, Mr Edwards,' Adele reassured him. 'Now would you like to sit on the cycle?'

'Used to do a lot of cycling in my younger days, Nurse— kept us fit—didn't hear of young folk having heart attacks and the like.'

'We tend to think of social changes as progress, don't we? But it's not all beneficial. More and more people are turning towards health clubs and vigorous sport to keep fit.

It is necessary where people do sitting down jobs or a lot of car travelling.'

Mr Edwards had seated himself on the cycle and Adele placed two fingers over the pulse on the wrist of his right hand, recording his pulse rate before he commenced pedalling.

'You have to keep this up for two minutes, so don't overdo it,' she advised. 'Just pedal at a steady pace.'

Using the stopwatch she clocked the two minutes and then took his pulse again, which was a much faster rate.

'Now two minutes' rest and we'll see how well you recover,' she explained.

Again using her stopwatch she waited a further two minutes before checking her client's pulse.

'Good,' she said as she recorded his recovery pulse-rate, 'that's exactly back to your resting pulse-rate.'

They passed on to the adjoining room where Adele helped Mr Edwards off with his shirt, and on to the couch.

'I won't bore you with explaining about the electrocardiogram as you obviously know what to expect, but we'll take your blood pressure first,' she said.

This was done several times in fact throughout each client's check-up, at differing stages as so often, especially in the case of clients visiting the clinic for the first time, anxiety caused blood-pressure readings to be higher than would normally be expected.

Adele watched the mercury level rise and fall again, then she removed the band from his arm and put the sphygmomanometer and stethoscope to one side.

From Mr Edwards's history she knew that together with his wife he ran a sizeable newsagent's shop in a town some seventy miles farther north.

'Have you driven down this morning, Mr Edwards?' she asked, as she smeared parts of his skin with a special lubricant necessary to ensure good contact when she attached him to the electro-cardiograph by means of wires and metal electrodes, a harmless, completely painless test.

'No, my dear,' he replied heartily. 'The business is still doing well, in spite of printers' strikes and industrial disputes generally. We're lucky to have a reliable woman who can manage for us, so we've taken a couple of days off. Stayed overnight in that nice hotel opposite here. That's why we're so calm and settled before we come to you. Besides,' he went on with a grin, 'me and the missus likes our grub—couldn't do a long journey on an empty stomach. Nothing to eat for fourteen hours before the checkup?—that's the hardest part for us. Can't wait to get back to the hotel restaurant for a good meal.'

'By which time I expect you'll find that your appetite has gone,' Adele warned him.

Mr Edwards laughed. 'Yes—but we'll make up for it this evening. We'll do the town, a bit of sight-seeing and maybe a night club while we're here, then take it easy driving back tomorrow.'

Adele indicated that she was ready to switch on. 'Tell me when you feel a pricking sensation in your arms, Mr Edwards.'

He nodded, and afterwards responded as she switched on the current, passing through two limbs only at a time. A few minutes later and Mr Edwards was able to replace his shirt.

Adele found him an easy person to chat with. It was, after all, his job, just as now it was hers to be as pleasant as possible to clients, and Mr Edwards, being a regular visitor to *A Votre Santé* Clinic, showed little sign of nervousness.

Before leaving that room Mr Edwards was required to blow into a tube attached to a special machine used for measuring lung capacity. This lung-function test usually precipitated some amusement, but after a couple of good exhalations a sound reading was recorded, proving in Mr Edwards's case that the vital capacity of his lungs was not reduced, as it would be if lung disease were present.

'Just sight and hearing tests and then it'll be your turn to see Dr Forbes,' Adele said as she escorted Mr Edwards across the lounge, through the double doors and along a passageway in the opposite direction from the reception area.

It was a fair-sized room with a visual testing card hung on

one wall and a revolutionary machine, the non-contact Tonometer which measures intra-ocular pressure set up on a side table. This test in conjunction with others would help the doctor to diagnose glaucoma, a serious eye disease, usually symptomless.

Part of this same room was divided off into two cubicles, one where Adele could observe her client through a window into the sound-proof cubicle as she recorded Mr Edwards's response by means of a buzzer to various pitches of sound transmitted by Adele to her client through an ear-piece.

Like most people, Mr Edwards could hear marginally better from one ear than the other, but for a man half-way to sixty years of age he was, as he had predicted, fairly fit as far as Adele could tell, but only the final results analysed by a doctor would confirm this.

With the test completed Adele led the way back to the lounge.

'Now I'm sure you're ready for that cup of coffee,' she said with a smile. 'Only two dry biscuits though, I'm afraid.'

Adele had no sooner made the coffee and handed it to her client than she heard voices in the passageway, so she went to meet Mrs Edwards who was smiling up at Dr Gavin Forbes, obviously flattered by his attention.

He shook hands with his patient before they reached the lounge.

'Adele will look after you now, Mrs Edwards, and I shall expect to see you in a year's time,' he said, turning to go back into his consulting room.

'I'm almost sorry that hour is over,' Mrs Edwards whispered to Adele confidentially. 'He's a really gorgeous man.' She was flushed but radiant, and Adele couldn't help wondering whether her client would feel the same about Dr Forbes if she had to live with him.

Coffee was already made in the lounge and Sheila served it.

'There we are, Mrs Edwards,' she said. 'You can have five minutes with your husband before we separate you again for round two.'

They were a devoted couple by all appearances, and eager to exchange their experiences of the past hour, so Adele took Mr Edwards's chart along to Dr Forbes, at the same time serving his coffee.

'Ah, Adele—a much needed stimulant.' He regarded her with a fixed, impenetrable stare, his cool green eyes gradually changing to a deeper shade as a mischievous sparkle warmed his expression. Without mentioning his client Adele knew that he was indicating that he found Mrs Edwards a trifle overpowering.

'And how did you find *Mr* Edwards?' he asked pointedly.

'On the whole very good—perhaps a little breathless from time to time,' she noted.

'The usual indication of a middle-age slowing down process—a charming, sensible couple though. You'll find Mrs Edwards very cooperative.'

His expression had reverted again to that indefinable disassociation. Adele found herself curious as to what went on in Gavin Forbes's head to create such rapid changes of mood and manner. He didn't mince his words, she had learned, and yet at the same time he exercised a clever economy with them. For a split second of time she thought she could imagine what was occupying his mind, and then as suddenly she realised that his thoughts were probably directing him along an entirely different route from her own.

Everyone held him in high esteem, particularly Mrs Edwards who, during the following hour sang his praises constantly so that Adele's diplomacy was tested thoroughly as she attempted to complete the necessary tests. At least Adele didn't have to mentally search for suitable topics of conversation. Mrs Edwards was only too eager to relate her life history, and because of Adele's novice status expound her knowledge of the running of the clinic.

The exercise-tolerance test took the wind out of her sails briefly, and after two minutes of cycling, followed by two minutes' rest, her recovery pulse-rate had not returned to her normal rate, but Adele recorded her findings without commenting, except to observe that Mrs Edwards was half a stone heavier than the previous year.

'It must be difficult having all those sweets and choco-lates to tempt you all the time,' Adele suggested.

'We hardly ever touch them,' Mrs Edwards assured her. 'In the early days we sickened ourselves, so it just doesn't bother us any more. For some reason this year I haven't lost those few pounds that inevitably go on around Christmas time. Middle-age spread I suppose, but if that's all I have to worry about I'm very lucky.'

'Everyone is very weight-conscious these days, but it pays to be sensible as overweight does put a strain on the heart.'

They had moved on to the next room now, and as Mrs Edwards reclined on the couch she seemed to study Adele closely.

'I had a nifty figure like yours when I was your age.' She laughed. 'I must ask Dr Forbes if he holds some sort of beauty contest to find his nurses—he certainly knows how to pick the most attractive girls with the dandiest of figures. Can't think why he always chooses married women though. He ought to be married, he's far too good to be wasted as a bachelor. Don't you wish you were free, Adele?'

Adele concentrated on attaching the electro-cardiograph wires to her client, at the same time feeling the strings of her own heart pull tighter, but she managed a faint laugh. 'In a way I suppose I am, Mrs Edwards. I'm a widow.'

'Oh—my dear—how thoughtless of me, but then, how could I possibly know?'

She was full of sympathy and curious to know the details which didn't help Adele, who was relieved when the screening was finally over and she could walk Mr and Mrs Edwards to the door.

Dr Forbes chose that moment to emerge from his office and Mrs Edwards grasped a last opportunity to take and hold his hand.

'Goodbye again, Dr Forbes,' she gushed. 'I was just telling Adele here that it's high time you got yourself married. All this super virility going to waste just isn't good enough, you know. And there's this harem of beautiful girls desperately trying to please you. You'll have to watch out,' she warned flippantly.

Gavin Forbes's confidence wavered slightly under her effusive display, and his glance met Adele's briefly before he recovered his composure.

'I shall indeed, Mrs Edwards,' he replied smoothly, 'but I do assure you that I pick my attractive girls with good intent.'

A wicked smile, a slightly raised eyebrow in provocative fashion as he gently, and almost unnoticed, slid his hand away from Mrs Edwards before continuing on his purposeful way.

A few minutes later Adele returned from the reception area to the waiting lounge to find Matthew chatting to Dr Forbes.

They both smiled in acknowledgement as she made to by-pass them, but a firm hand restrained her.

'Perhaps we can persuade this fair damsel to make us some coffee,' Dr Forbes said, turning to walk beside her, with Matthew on her other side.

'She's the expert,' Matthew assured his friend, and Adele was aware of them exchanging glances over her head.

'I haven't had the chance of a chat during your first few days, Adele,' Dr Forbes went on gently. 'I expect you were about to have coffee yourself so let's go and sit down for a few moments.'

Adele glanced over her shoulder towards him.

'Shall I bring it over?' she asked, and he inclined his head in agreement.

She was glad of a few moments to allow the blush to fade as she made the coffee and prepared everything on a tray, but it was with a rather unsteady hand that she carried it to a far corner which the two doctors had chosen.

'Oh dear,' she rebuked herself sharply, 'I'm afraid I've spilt it.'

'Sit down—and for heaven's sake stop looking so worried,' Dr Forbes cut in impatiently.

Adele stole a glance at Matthew and observed his pale

blue eyes mischievously laughing at her as she sat on the
edge of the orange corner unit couches.

'Now, fair damsel, what have you got to say for yourself?'
her employer demanded.

'N . . . nothing,' Adele stammered, feeling acutely be-
wildered.

Matthew sat back on the next couch, his long arm
spanning the back, and crossing his legs he leaned slightly
towards her.

'How have you been, my dear?' he asked.

'Fine, thanks,' she answered in a mild voice, thinking
ungraciously that a lot he cared, judging by his absence
over the past few days.

'I purposely didn't telephone, I felt you needed time to
yourselves,' he explained softly.

'And how's that young son of yours?' Gavin Forbes
enquired sternly.

'Oh, fine, fine,' Adele blurted, wishing that she had the
courage to do today what she had promised herself to do
tomorrow.

Gavin helped himself generously to the cream and then,
to Adele's surprise, filled her cup to the brim.

'You'll need a straw,' Matthew commented laughing
heartily and she was aware again of the two men exchanging unvoiced conversation.

'Perhaps that will encourage you to tell the truth,' Gavin
said in a more sombre voice. 'You haven't been sleeping
well, you don't eat and you don't quite understand what is
happening to you.'

Adele looked from Matthew to Gavin, and back to
Matthew again, her liquid eyes begging for help.

'No, Adele, I will not accept your resignation.' At this
she gasped. 'You will stick it out for a month and by that
time you'll be grateful to Matthew and myself for being
ruthless.'

'You're that, certainly,' Adele managed in a croaky
whisper.

'Now, about Oliver.' Gavin chose to ignore her opinion
of himself.

'What about Oliver?' she asked meekly.

'No tantrums?'

Adele shook her head. 'Quite the reverse—I can hardly get him to say a word.'

'That's normal,' Gavin said. 'Wouldn't you agree, Matthew?'

Oh, how hateful these men were, and Adele felt her animosity growing. How could they possibly know? Bachelors with only textbook knowledge to guide them.

'It will take a little while, Adele,' Matthew said kindly.

'Two weeks to be exact,' Gavin informed her.

'Children aren't all alike,' she managed to whisper.

'Experience has shown, and don't forget that millions of children have to go to school and face these first traumatic days, that on average it takes two weeks for a young child to accept a new pattern. I'm quite confident that Oliver will be no exception.' He paused and indicated her overflowing cup of coffee. 'Having dealt with Oliver how do you like our clinic?'

At that moment she was wondering how to manage an overfull cup. She wanted to retort 'not very much', but her subconscious rejected her stubbornness, and she truthfully agreed that she was impressed.

To the men's amusement she succeeded in getting cup and saucer close to her mouth and defiantly took the first few sips without slopping coffee everywhere.

There were a few moments of boisterous merriment and Adele, with burning cheeks, replaced her cup and saucer on the tray.

'Congratulations,' Gavin said, with still more spontaneous laughter. 'A steady hand and determined spirit.'

Matthew ran a slender finger up her cheek, and said confidentially: 'He rates himself as something of a psychiatrist, that was just his way of putting you to the test.'

'Then I hope I passed,' Adele managed light-heartedly.

Gavin raised his eyebrows, half-smiled, and then became stern-faced again, intimating that the frivolity had ended.

'There are one or two things I'd like to mention, and the first is that I like my girls to avail themselves of our services, so I've arranged for a colleague to come over next week for your consultation. It wouldn't be prudent, of course, for any of us to act as your consultant. Sheila will take you round on all the other tests which I suggest you fit in between now and next Wednesday. There's the little matter of the lengthy questionnaire. Would it be too much to ask you to take it home today, and get it filled up? Then I can let Dr Hill-Stevens have it to study over the weekend.'

Adele was aware of the other nurses hovering in the background. Some patients leaving, others just arriving, so she stood up quickly.

'No, Adele,' Gavin said shortly. 'I have not given you permission to leave, and if you were thinking of saying that you don't need a medical screening save your breath. As your employer I insist, and as you are a qualified nursing sister you know it is sensible.'

Adele stared down at him, the colour in her cheeks a sign of annoyance. Mostly because he had anticipated her reaction so correctly. A change of attitude was necessary so she replied airily: 'I thought I ought to get back to work.'

'Sit down,' he commanded, and when she had complied he continued: 'I expect you know that incorporated with the clinic we have a health and beauty club. Ideal for would-be slimmers, though that doesn't apply to you, but under our instructor's supervision a body building programme will be devised in your case. You'll find regular exercises followed by sauna baths will help you to relax completely. Added to which a good diet will assist in keeping you fit.'

'It sounds very nice for the people who like that kind of thing, but I'm afraid I wouldn't be able to go in for that—because of Oliver,' she added pointedly.

'We've thought of that.' He met her questioning stare with pertinacity. 'You can bring Oliver back here after lunch on occasion, there's always someone free to keep an eye on him, or Matthew is offering to baby-sit sometimes in the evenings.'

'But I couldn't be such a nuisance to other people,' Adele said hurriedly, amazed at the speed and efficiency with which Dr Gavin Forbes appeared to have taken her over.

'You don't have a choice, Adele,' Gavin responded clearly, and stood up abruptly.

Adele gulped down her protestations and standing found herself gazing levelly at her new boss.

'You may go and greet your next patients,' he directed, and with a brief glance at Matthew, Adele left the men to their plotting.

She had walked half-way across the floor when Gavin Forbes called her back. He held the tray towards her. 'Yours to dispose of, I think.'

She coloured guiltily—was it possible for her cheeks to burn to explosion point?—and cursed herself for not remembering the tray.

At the small sink beneath the coffee bar Denise sidled up to her as Adele washed the cups and saucers, giving vent to her anger.

'A Mr and Mrs Hathaway in reception for you—but don't rush, they're early.'

Her own personal feelings had to be thrust aside as she greeted her clients pleasantly, and when she had escorted Mrs Hathaway to Matthew's consulting room she took Mr Hathaway to the various rooms for tests.

Her indignation quickly abated as interest in her work occupied her fully until it was time to leave.

Sheila handed her a thick envelope. 'That will keep you busy for the rest of today,' she laughed.

Adele made a face. 'I wish I didn't have to,' she began.

Sheila waved a finger at her. 'No good protesting. Dr Forbes believes you can't sell this to your clients if you haven't experienced it yourself. He's right, or course, as well we all know. Make the most of the free offer in case you don't like us enough to stay.'

Adele took the envelope grudgingly and hesitated before taking Sheila up on her remark.

'It wouldn't be because I don't like it here, or the staff,' she said urgently.

'Take a tip from me, Adele, you could do a lot worse. We're all ex-hospital sisters and loved our work, but you have to admit that there are a lot of pressures in hospitals, and it's not easy to cope with them *and* a husband—*and* children, as well as running a home.'

'I hadn't thought of returning to hospital,' Adele said cautiously. 'Not for years, anyway.'

'But in your circumstances you have to do something— *you're* the breadwinner—oh, social security helps, but it isn't enough if you want to give your son a decent living, besides, it's so much better for you to go out and mix. That's one good thing about this job, you have time to talk to the clients, and some of them are jolly interesting. Don't give up too easily, Adele.'

'Who said I was ready to quit?'

Sheila was several years older than Adele, tall and elegant, the kind of woman whom Gavin Forbes would choose to take command in his absence, the sophisticated type who matched his conventions.

She smiled readily. 'It has shown in every look, almost every word, but Gavin won't let you quit unless he wants you to.'

'If I chose not to come in,' Adele suggested hesitantly.

'He'd probably go and fetch you. He's a very possessive man and there's more to it than just being one of his staff. Believe me, Adele, beneath his austere manner he really cares, and I should know, I've been with him since he opened this clinic.'

Adele fingered the envelope in her hand and somehow couldn't bring herself to say how she hated leaving Oliver. It wasn't that Sheila and the other girls didn't understand, but it was beginning to sound like her theme-song. They evidently thought it was of financial necessity for Adele to work, it wasn't, but perhaps it was best to keep that to herself.

Adele had mixed feelings on Friday when she realised that this was the day she had intended to give in her notice. Dr Forbes though had made it abundantly clear that he meant her to keep her side of the bargain. He couldn't force her to, of course, but she must be fair for Matthew's sake. She did enjoy talking to her clients and doing the more technical side of the work like labelling the blood samples and packaging them up to go off to London for analysis, as well as collecting all the results when they were returned, and checking patients' files ready for the various examining doctors to prepare their reports, so that she quickly forgot her resolve.

Half way through the morning, when she went to reception to greet her second clients of the day, she almost collided with Dr Forbes coming out of his office. She was brought up sharply by the presence of a woman at his side. Tall, smartly dressed, Adele sensed at once that she was not just another client. The blue-eyed, dark-haired elegantly sophisticated woman was *his* woman! Adele had no time to assess the relationship, she just knew that there was a togetherness, a closeness which married them just as surely as if they were man and wife.

'Ah, Adele.' Dr Forbes dropped his arm from his companion's waist. 'I've just been checking over the results of yesterday's tests on Mr and Mrs Edwards. Do you usually write so small?'

The colour rushed into Adele's cheeks.

'I . . . well, yes . . . I try to be neat,' she replied honestly.

She caught a glimpse of the sarcastic smile again, and how she hated Gavin Forbes as he added cryptically: 'I shall need a magnifying glass to study your test results if you continue to write so spidery.'

Spidery! How dare he be so rude?

'I'm sorry,' she heard herself saying. 'No one's ever complained before.' She was on the point of reminding him that she had been a ward sister up to the time of her pregnancy, but she kept herself in check. He knew all about her previous career and by the nonchalant grin she guessed that he was deliberately finding fault to draw her attention to the fact that he had a lady friend in spite of all that Mrs Edwards had insinuated. How childish, Adele thought.

'Far be it from me to complain, Adele,' Gavin Forbes continued, 'being neat is one thing, trying my eyesight another. It would make my job easier if you could make your findings legible.'

'I'll try to remember,' Adele offered and went on to the reception area. At least his woman had been thoughtful enough to walk on during her reprimand. Adele felt her nerves on edge. She hadn't liked him from the start, now she considered him petty. No doubt he would find plenty of other causes for complaint as time went on. He would compile a dossier on her she supposed and at some future date would take her to task over minor misdemeanours.

For the remainder of the morning Adele couldn't get the woman out of her mind. She remembered Mrs Edwards suggesting that Dr Forbes ought to be married, and that he must watch out. He had replied that he chose his girls with good intent. Of course he did, they were all married so he hoped this woman of his would not see any association with his staff as a threat. But Adele was a widow. How did his lady friend view that, she wondered? If only she knew, Adele reflected angrily, she was welcome to him. No way would Adele tolerate such an ambiguous pig. Her thoughts ran riot. He had rebuked her over a triviality deliberately in front of his female companion in order to put her off, as well as indicating to Adele that he wasn't free. The conceit of it! As if she cared one way or another!

At the end of the morning, just before she went home, Adele's opinion of his relationship with the woman was confirmed. Screenings ended often at a simultaneous time so that clients, doctors and nurses all converged to the waiting lounge.

It appeared that the woman had been taken round on the tests by Sheila, and her consultation with the examining doctor, Dr Chesterfield, had just come to an end.

Gavin Forbes had his arm reassuringly across the woman's shoulders as Dr Chesterfield said goodbye and left.

'Do you need to freshen up before we go to lunch?' Gavin asked his friend.

'Food—or rather a drink first, darling,' the woman answered seductively, and they left the clinic close in conversation.

Adele went to pick up Oliver, angry with herself for feeling needled. What difference did his private life make to her?

CHAPTER THREE

'WHAT shall we do this afternoon, darling?' Adele asked Oliver as she washed up their Sunday dinner things.

'Could we go on that hill?'

She looked down at his upturned, trusting face, fearful for a moment that he meant the crematorium where they often took flowers.

'Where Daddy flied the kite,' he said solemnly.

Adele laughed. 'Have we still got the kite?' she asked, having long forgotten such adventures.

'Daddy hung it in the garage—I can fetch it,' Oliver assured her.

Adele dried her hands and unlocked the garage door at one end of the spacious kitchen. She only went into the garage when it was absolutely necessary, because the sight of Bernie's new Volvo standing so lifeless, still shiny and new, seemed to taunt her. Oliver pushed past her, seemingly unconcerned at the sight of the car, and pointed up to a shelf in the long row of shelves which Bernie had built. Adele knew she would have to come to a decision about the car, it was silly to leave her own outside in the drive when there was ample space for two in the garage. It was just that she found the sight of the Volvo a reminder of dreams crashing to the ground.

Oliver tugged her hand and she found a pair of steps to stand on, enabling her to reach the kite.

It wasn't until later when they had parked the car in the general car park and walked along a narrow track up the side of the hill to the grassy plateau at the top that Adele realised her own inadequacy.

'Darling, I'm sorry,' she said as Oliver began to unwind the string on the bobbins, 'I don't think I know what to do.'

'I'll show you, Mummy,' he said proudly. 'I have to run with the kite and you must pull on the strings—you can let it out like Daddy did.'

Adele felt her nose reddening with the keen wind, and it whipped right through her black cords and black velvet jacket, but somehow she had to attempt to master this kite flying.

Fortunately no one else was in the spot she had chosen and undoing a length of the string Oliver began to run. Adele hadn't given any thought to the direction of the wind, but Oliver had made off with it and the kite was snatched out of his hand into the air. Adele felt the cords tugging and she heard Oliver's shrieks of delight which suddenly changed into screams of terror as a dog's barking reached her ears.

A shout brought the animal to a halt and then she found she was enclosed in a man's arms as he took control of the kite. She was forced to lean back against a masculine chest and a familiar voice crooned in her ear.

'Just as well I happened along, fair damsel, or you might have gone soaring off into space. There's a strong wind today, and there's not enough of you to stand against a puff.'

'I've never done it before,' Adele gasped, 'but Oliver wanted to—'

'Bob down under my arms and hang on to Honey, my dog, then call Oliver here—I'll teach him—' but Oliver was already there, panting as he anxiously appraised this long-legged man who was being familiar with his Mum.

'This is Dr Forbes, darling,' Adele whispered. 'Uncle Matthew's friend from the clinic where I work.'

'Come along and hold the reels, Oliver,' Gavin said. 'You're a clever chap getting it up first time.'

But Oliver buried his face in Adele's side and she felt his small body quivering with sobs.

'It's all right, sweetheart,' she consoled. 'Did the dog frighten you?'

'She won't hurt you, Oliver,' Gavin said decisively. 'Her name is Honey, and when you ran she thought you wanted to play.' The wind carried his voice away and he had to battle with the controls of the kite.

'Look, darling, it's up so high,' Adele said to take his

mind off the dog, and Oliver smudged his face with his hands and stood transfixed at the antics of the kite, especially its long colourful tail.

'Come on, Oliver, come and help me to hold it,' Gavin called after a few minutes, and Oliver went to him eagerly.

Adele watched, then turned her attention to Honey who was surveying her master with interest. She was a golden retriever with delectable blue eyes and alert ears. Adele bent down and smoothed her fine coat and immediately Honey lifted her paw to greet Adele.

The kite stayed up well, fluttering and prancing in the currents of wind and Gavin and Oliver achieved a great height until their arms were tired and Gavin brought it down.

'Did you see, Mummy? I did it too,' Oliver said excitedly, running back towards her, but seeing Honey he paused.

'It's all right, Oliver, she's very friendly, she only wants to play.'

Adele went forward and had difficulty in controlling Oliver as he twisted round and round her legs to get away from Honey who was eager to make friends.

'Honey—sit!' Gavin commanded.

By now Adele was shivering with the cold as she waited for Gavin to return the kite. He wound up the string, but he didn't return it to Adele, instead he carefully laid it on the grass, then he stooped beside Honey and beckoned to Oliver.

'Come along, young man, she wants to be your friend, come and stroke her head.'

Oliver still clung to Adele as she urged him forward.

'I bet you don't do what your Mummy tells you as quickly as Honey sat down for me.'

Gavin was smiling and caught Oliver in his arm, gently lifting his hand and placing it on Honey's head.

'Now, Honey,' Gavin said. 'What do you say to Oliver for frightening him—don't you think you should say sorry?'

Honey took a moment to consider this request then stretched out on the grass and with one paw gently pawed Oliver's shoes.

'Now say "Hullo",' Gavin ordered, and Honey sat up in a begging position, 'and, "how do you do",' and she obediently offered her paw to Oliver. Gavin placed Oliver's hand round the dog's paw and he chuckled with glee, obviously impressed.

Gavin went on to make a fuss of the dog, found a stone and threw it, then gave Oliver a ball from his pocket and soon Honey and Oliver were playing together happily. Gavin turned his attention to Adele.

'Evidently you don't have any pets?' he said.

Adele smiled. 'No. Bernie felt they are best suited to the country, and I agreed with him. We did consider it when we first moved to Beecroft, but then Bernie was taken ill, so—' she shrugged.

Gavin was gazing at her intently. 'You're frozen stiff, girl. You should be wearing a thicker coat up here,' he admonished, but with a friendly smile.

'It's colder than I realised,' she answered, and felt her cheeks flush with embarrassment as his green eyes travelled down the length of her and up again.

Was he finding her outfit significant? Should she explain that she liked black, that Bernie had liked her to look tall and slim, and that she'd bought this particular jacket and cords two years ago?

'My God, Adele, it's time someone took you in hand. Whatever can Matthew be thinking of, you need a tonic, building up.'

Now, she rebelled. 'I'm perfectly fit. All you doctors have health on the brain,' she retorted indignantly.

'That's right.' He was laughing at her rebellion. 'It's our job. *A Votre Santé*, my dear fair damsel.' Then his face darkened. 'Be sensible, Adele, you have Oliver to consider. When you've grieved yourself into your grave who will care for your son?'

Adele lifted her head defiantly, but people were walking by so she refrained from further argument, instead she looked round for Oliver.

Gavin followed her gaze briefly. 'He's all right. Doing me a favour in fact, wearing Honey out.' But Oliver was

moving farther away as he persistently threw the ball for
Honey which the dog retrieved and returned to place at
Oliver's feet. Gavin placed his arm round Adele's shoulder
and together they walked towards Oliver. 'When did you
last hold an intelligent conversation with anyone which
didn't concern Oliver?' he asked gently.

'Oliver is all I have,' Adele stated firmly. 'Would you
have me neglect him?'

'Now you're being absurd, and over-obsessed with your
responsibility. You are young too; too young to bury your
head in the sand and pretend you don't have a life apart
from Oliver. When he grows up—and they do you know—
you'll wake up to the fact that life has passed you by, and
you'll have no one but yourself to blame. Besides, possessive mothers do untold harm to their children.'

'I'm hardly being over-possessive caring for my son
who's only four years old. The first five years of a child's life
are the formative years, the years that count,' Adele
argued.

'That's right—so gradually you have to introduce a measure of independence now, and that's where the nursery
school will prove to be a splendid sounding board. But I'm
not concerned about Oliver. You have a son to be proud of,
Adele. He's a normal, happy little boy. It's his Mum I'm
worried about.'

'There's really no need for you to be,' she said, suddenly
confused by the pressure of his arm round her shoulder,
which even as she glanced up at him slid down to her waist.
She felt his fingers searching for her body.

'Look at this,' he said, pausing to gather up a handful of
spare coat. 'There's nothing of you—you're all skin and
bone.'

Embarrassed she pulled out of his reach, but he caught
her to him in what she supposed was a paternal manner.

'I don't intend to let you waste away to dust. I like my
staff to be a good advertisement for my clinic, they must be
an example of excellent health.'

Adele opened her mouth to speak—to say that she was
evidently in the wrong job by his criticisms, but the pressure

of his fingers dallying at her tiny waist took her breath away and she was obliged to wriggle away from him, her eyes bright, her cheeks glowing. In twisting away she noticed the tail of the kite flapping on the ground.

'The kite!' she cried and began to run back. She picked it up and walked slowly across the grassy plateau to where Gavin had joined Oliver and Honey. He threw the ball to Oliver who inveigled Adele to joining in a game of catch.

Slowly they were working their way down the hill and several times Adele had to return for the kite so that by the time they neared the car park again she was quite breathless.

'Next time we'll play football,' Gavin promised Oliver.

'We've got one in the car,' Oliver responded enthusiastically and Adele had to laugh as she exchanged glances with Gavin, thinking that it served him right.

'Only a quick game then,' Adele said to Oliver as she opened up the hatchback, 'it's time to go home.'

Gavin ordered Honey to sit by Adele's car while he limbered up and enjoyed a boisterous game with Oliver which ended with roust-about horse-play on the grass until Oliver was laughing infectiously. And then it was all over and Gavin saying he must take Honey home.

'Couldn't Honey come to my house to tea?' Oliver asked, suddenly serious, looking up into Gavin's face, his dark eyes enormous, and appealing.

Adele felt her energy fading. Now there would be trouble to get Oliver home, she supposed.

'Does that invitation extend to me?' Gavin asked with a smile.

Adele put the ball into the rear of the car along with the kite, and Oliver pulled at her jacket.

'I expect Dr Forbes has other things to do, darling.'

'I'm pleased to say I have nothing else to do today, and after such energetic exercise a cup of tea would be most welcome.'

Adele looked round. 'Don't you have your car?'

He shook his head, a wicked smile reflected in his taunting eyes which seemed to be claiming having got one over on Adele.

'I was out walking the dog,' he said.

'Well, of course, you're welcome to come and have a cup of tea if you really want to.'

She hadn't meant to sound rude, but the tone of her voice did imply that she thought he had a cheek to invite himself, and heavens what could she give him to eat? Adele had grown accustomed to supplying Oliver's needs and little else.

'Do you object to having Honey in the rear?' Gavin asked, and already Oliver was hassling the dog to get up into the car.

'You can sit by my ball,' he explained to Honey and then climbed in the rear passenger seat where he could kneel up and lean over the back to be near Honey.

Gavin closed the hatchback saying: 'I'll get in with Oliver so that you can concentrate on your driving,' and inwardly Adele heaved a sigh of relief.

As they drove into the wide tarmacadamed driveway Gavin leaned over the front passenger seat.

'I didn't realise you lived so far out of town.'

Adele undid her seat belt, remembering her first morning at the clinic.

'It isn't really far,' she replied off-handedly, then glancing over her shoulder was obliged to smile. 'I'm afraid you must be a bit cramped back there.'

He smiled in return, but the expression in his green eyes told Adele that he was remembering too, and she wondered as she got out of the car if he felt a moment's remorse at having a go at her on her first morning. He was squeezing himself out of the other side so Adele opened up the hatchback and Oliver scrambled over the back of the seat and got out with Honey.

'Can I open the garage door for you?' Gavin asked.

Adele was already walking towards the front door, she half-turned. 'I usually leave it there.'

'Why?' Gavin asked pointedly.

Adele shrugged and in an instant Gavin was behind her demanding a reply.

'I just do,' she said, pushing open the front door.

Gavin held her arm. 'Not so fast—is there a way to the garden through the garage—I expect you'd like Honey to stay outside.'

'There is—but I don't mind Honey coming in, and I'm sure Oliver will insist on it.'

Gavin walked back from the verandah which sheltered the glass panel and front door on to the circular lawn. He gazed up at the house interested in the detail of design.

Adele stood on the threshold waiting, feeling it right that she should do so, while Oliver busily closed the wrought iron gates to keep Honey inside.

'I'm most impressed,' Gavin said following Adele into the house. 'It's very large and you have extra rooms over the garage I see,' he observed.

Adele slipped off her jacket and hung it on the elegant hall stand.

'I'll show you over the house after tea if you'd like to see it,' she invited. 'We have a self-contained flat over a double garage,' she explained, then laughed. 'Bernie had big ideas, but what architect doesn't have? We laughingly called it our "granny flat" but he really built it with our children in mind. He was a great one for thinking ahead, for being futuristic, and he had ultra-modern ideas.'

'I can see that at a glance.'

Gavin had removed his jacket too, revealing grey flannels perfectly tailored with a thick sweater in varying shades of blue. He looked less formal, more cosy with his neck hidden by the polo collar.

Adele shivered, and hurried into the lounge where at the touch of a switch the gas fire came to life.

'Please, do sit down,' she said turning to Gavin. 'Will you excuse me if I go and find something warmer to put on?'

His eyes were a sparkling green now and as they flitted over her thin shirt blouse she knew he liked what he saw.

'If you must,' he said softly, his gaze directed at the

points of her small breasts which showed through the otherwise ill-fitting blouse. 'Attractive though it is, you're a foolish girl to go out half-dressed.'

Adele hurried out of the room. There seemed little point in repeating that she hadn't realised that the wind was so cold. She paused at the front door to call Oliver inside and then she went up to her bedroom. She looked at herself in the mirror as she undid her blouse. It was true there wasn't much of her but the curves were all there if only in miniature. A sudden urge gave her a desire to look feminine. It was Sunday, and perhaps Dr Gavin Forbes was old-fashioned and liked women to have a 'best' dress. As she wriggled out of the cords she opened her wardrobe door and surveyed its contents. A row of beautiful garments that had held little interest for her over recent weeks, now she pulled down a dress of emerald green recalling that she had bought it as a treat for herself for losing some weight once. It was made in jersey crimplene, in a style that had clung and fitted to her full, moulded bustline. A slightly flared skirt hung from the small waist but the pounds had soon crept on again so that the dress had quickly been discarded. Now, Adele put on a slip and then the dress, finding that it fitted easily, even a trifle loosely, but it felt warm and comfortable. She pinned a diamond brooch to one shoulder, an expensive piece of jewellery which Bernie had given to her when Oliver was born. She looked in the mirror again, touching up her face with make-up, combing her shoulder-length honey-coloured hair so that it sprang into natural waves and curls. She wanted to look nice. But why, she asked the reflection in the mirror? It isn't Bernie waiting downstairs to take you in his arms to hug and kiss you, it's Dr Gavin Forbes, your employer, and he already has a woman. Should she start again and go back to the cords and a thick sweater? No, she was being too long, he had invited himself to come and have a cup of tea so she must go and entertain her guest.

She went down the wide staircase into the lounge and found it empty. Then she followed voices into the kitchen and was surprised to see Gavin buttering bread, while

Oliver, kneeling on a chair, was fitting ham between the slices.

Gavin looked up, knife poised, as he took in the transformation.

'Expecting someone?' he asked flippantly.

'No—'

'Uncle Matthew presently,' Oliver put in helpfully.

'You shouldn't be doing this,' Adele said tying an apron round her.

'Oliver assured me that this was the menu. We've both washed our hands, and I'm afraid Honey has commandeered the rug in front of the fire.'

Adele laughed. 'I'm sorry, I'm afraid I only cater for Oliver and me.'

'Then you'd better start catering for an army, fair damsel, because between us, Matthew and I mean to see you're eating properly. What did you have for lunch?'

If Oliver hadn't been present Adele would probably have told him not to be so inquisitive, but how could you win with an honest four year old?

'Chops,' she answered, simply.

'And I had sausages, and baked beans too,' Oliver added eagerly.

'What else did Mummy have?' Gavin asked Oliver.

'A potato.' He shook his head. 'Daddy said she mustn't eat too much 'cos he liked her to be cuddly.'

'There soon won't be much left to cuddle,' Gavin said jovially.

Oliver looked up from the sandwiches he was making. 'I love my Mummy, and *I* cuddle her now Daddy's gone.'

'Isn't anyone else allowed to?' Gavin asked with a disappointed frown.

Oliver returned to his task thoughtfully. 'Well,' he said slowly, 'Uncle Matthew does *some*times—but you could if you liked,' he conceded generously.

Adele turned away. 'What shall I do?' she asked a little too brightly.

'Apart from being available for cuddles? Lay up, where-

ver you eat?' Gavin suggested, and Adele was thankful to
leave the kitchen.

She set out dainty china cups, saucers and plates and
surprised herself at the length of time which had passed
since they had been taken out of the china cabinet. Over
four months, she remembered, on the day of Bernie's
funeral. Even poor Matthew had been delegated a certain
mug from the pinewood Welsh dresser in the kitchen since
then. She ought to entertain for Oliver's sake, it was after
all part of his education, but who was there to entertain? It
wasn't that she didn't have friends, that she didn't keep in
touch. Adele sighed, realising with some self-reproach that
it was they who kept in touch with her by telephone.

A light step on the parquet flooring of the dining area
brought her back to the fact that Gavin was in the room. He
clicked his fingers in front of her eyes and laughed, and
came to stand close to her side, one arm round her waist.

'Sorry about the cuddles,' he teased gently. 'Little boys
of four years old aren't discreet enough not to mention such
nostalgic pastimes, so perhaps a little squeeze will keep you
going until Matthew gets here.'

He charmed a little laughter from her and then requested
a plate on which to put the sandwiches.

With pink cheeks Adele turned to the long, low side-
board and found a plate to match the tea-set, and a couple
of spare ones.

'I'm sorry it's only a light afternoon tea,' she apologised
again.

'I came for a cup of tea.' He paused, and looked embar-
rassingly long into her deep brown liquid eyes. 'Just being
in your company is a pleasure, Adele,' he added softly.

Thrown off balance she turned from the table and almost
dropped the plates, but hurried back to the kitchen. She
made the tea and called Oliver. By now he was constantly at
Gavin's side and he led the doctor to the table.

'Him—him can sit in Daddy's place,' Oliver stated,
granting his new friend an honoured liberty, but Gavin
helped him into his chair and said: 'Can't I sit next to you?'

Adele had already placed the extra plate at the opposite

end of the table to herself, now Gavin moved Oliver up closer to Adele, so that there was room on the same side of the oblong table for him.

This was going to be the most embarrassing mealtime of her life, she thought, but Gavin Forbes was a master of social conversation, and she had to admit that he had a way with Oliver that made Matthew seem a most inexperienced Uncle.

Adele almost got to wishing that he would stay for the evening, but of course she had to get rid of him somehow before Matthew arrived, and that wouldn't be until after Oliver's bedtime.

When Oliver was all ready for bed he insisted that 'him' should piggy-back him upstairs, and Adele took this opportunity to show Gavin over the rest of the house. Now he would go, he must, she decided, but when they returned to the lounge he strode to the aluminium double glazed french windows, unlocked them and ordered Honey outside. The evenings were drawing in and already dusk was enclosing the garden in a damp net. Gavin stepped outside and took the dog across the patio away from the house. Exasperated and with one eye on the clock Adele returned to the kitchen and started to wash up. She listened to the sound of the french windows closing, the soft but decisive tread of her boss walking across the lounge, the hall and into the kitchen. She felt nervousness enveloping her. How could she tell him to go? A polite way of dismissing him, and his wretched dog, Honey, simply refused to present itself! And, after all, it was hardly her place to remind him that somewhere his lady friend might be expecting him!

CHAPTER FOUR

ADELE kept her gaze firmly on the washing-up water as she heard him come up behind her. Lack of attention would surely indicate the cold shoulder, but she jumped in alarm when he slapped her on the rump quite sharply.

'Tea-cloth, fair damsel,' he demanded curtly.

Her cheeks blazed, this was going just too far. She swung round, facing him fearlessly.

'Dr Forbes!' she began.

He didn't move, but let her eyes level with his, then he grabbed her two hands, forced them behind her back and held them with one hand, the other hand clamped roughly over her mouth.

'Gavin,' he whispered seductively. 'It isn't that hard to say, surely?' He smiled wickedly at her struggles. 'I'm far too familiar? Is that what you wanted to say? You're a lovely girl, Adele, you have a charming son, a beautiful home—are you going to sacrifice all that should be normal to erect a shrine for Bernie? Everything about this home tells me that it echoed with happiness and laughter. I'm sorry to sound cruel, but don't you think your husband would like to look down and see that at least you were trying to be happy for Oliver's sake?'

She was struggling for breath, her eyes widening, her cheeks expanding as he gazed at her.

'If you're going to yell at me, I shall . . .' he paused, and moved in closer. 'I shall kiss you,' he said, moving his hand, but at that moment the door chimes interrupted, causing a mere flutter of his fair eyebrows.

'How *dare* you?' Adele said angrily, and Honey barked as the chimes ding-donged for the second time.

'I dare,' Gavin scoffed, 'for lots of reasons.' He let go her hands and chucked her under her chin. 'Don't keep Matthew waiting.'

Adele rubbed her wrists and actually ground her teeth at this infuriating man until they hurt. Wait till Matthew hears, she thought, rushing to the door, but as Matthew entered saying: 'Sorry, my dear, were you upstairs settling Oliver?' she knew she wouldn't tell anyone of the incident.

'Ah-ha!' Matthew said as Honey bounded up to him. 'What's this?—what are you doing here, Honey?'

With a lop-sided smug, self-satisfied grin Gavin strolled from the kitchen.

'Hullo, Matthew, I'm waiting to be given a cloth to dry up for my delectable hostess. We met up on the hill. Oliver tired both me and Honey out. We've been revived with tea so now I'm doing my share of the chores.'

'There's no need, Dr Forbes, really, I can do it,' Adele said hastily.

But he followed her into the kitchen again, leaving Matthew in the hall making a fuss of Honey and as Adele plunged her hands back into the washing-up water Gavin put his hand round her middle letting it slide down to her thigh as his lips tickled her ear.

'Are you going to double-dare me to embarrass Matthew?' he crooned, and his lips against her skin made her tingle. 'I could force you into using my Christian name, you know, but I'd rather you do it voluntarily.' She shook her head so that her silky hair fell across his face, but he only laughed and ran his fingers through it. 'The cloth, fair damsel or you'll provoke me to doing something we may both regret.'

'Oooh!' Adele groaned and impatiently reached for the clean tea-towel hanging between two kitchen units, which she then almost threw at him.

Honey came to investigate and Matthew stood at the doorway leaning against the architrave.

'So, you've had some company, my dear?' he said.

The slight hint of—what was it, annoyance? jealousy? sarcasm? Whatever it was jarred on Adele's nerves but she answered steadily: 'It was nice for Oliver to have someone who could fly the kite.'

'I think I just arrived in time to prevent Adele from being whisked heavenward,' Gavin said and his ill-chosen words added to Adele's confusion.

'Look at this,' Gavin went on, now in his element at teasing her. He pinched her waist making her twist from side to side. 'Very out of condition.'

'Oh, I don't know, you don't want to be plump again, do you, my dear?' Matthew said bluntly.

Adele wrung out the dish cloth, giving vent to her indignation. Men seemed to have no tact at all, she thought. 'If you don't mind, I don't like having my person discussed, and I'm probably in better condition than either of you,' she finished flatly.

'We'll soon find out when we see the results of your tests, and when we get you in the gym,' Gavin assured her.

'I don't have time for that sort of thing,' she mumbled as she packed the crockery on a tray and waited for Matthew to stand aside from the door.

'Perhaps you'd like a drink,' she said looking up at him, 'and I expect Dr Forbes would like one before he goes,' she added pointedly.

'And you?' Matthew asked with a wistful smile.

'No thanks, not just now, Matthew.'

As Adele put the things away, returned the tray to the kitchen and crept upstairs to make sure Oliver was settled she was aware of clinking glasses and lowered voices. She visited the bathroom, tidied her hair and decided that so much excitement was all too much for her. Gavin Forbes, she determined was a might too pushing, and in future would not be a welcome visitor to Beecroft. She paused at the top of the stairs wishing she had the courage to tell them both she wanted to be alone. It had been good to see Oliver chuckling again, and she was pleased that Gavin Forbes had been impressed by him, but she wasn't pleased at the way he was taking her over.

First Matthew, now Gavin. She was in a vulnerable position and would have to assert herself against these men who wanted to dominate.

When she returned to the lounge both men stood up

politely, and Adele's authoritative intentions dissolved into nothing.

'Sherry, my dear?' Matthew was the first to reach the drinks' cabinet.

'No,' she shook her head, 'no, I don't think so.'

'I insist,' Matthew said. 'Gavin and I don't want to drink alone.'

Drink, damn you, and go, she thought, but knew that if they did she would face yet another long lonely evening.

'That's *too* much, Matthew,' she scolded as he handed her the large schooner filled to the brim. 'You're doing this deliberately, just as Dr Forbes overfilled my coffee cup the other day.'

She took a couple of sips to prevent it from spilling over as she walked to the other recliner chair.

'Who is this Dr Forbes?' Gavin said facetiously, and a glance at him sprawled across the long settee filled her with awe. 'What do I have to do to make you less formal, Adele?' He actually sounded quite hurt.

'You are my employer,' she said huskily.

'From Monday to Friday, and mornings only. I make no attempt to mix business with pleasure,' he assured her, but Adele was not convinced. She was going to find working with him almost intolerable now.

The two men chatted, trying to include Adele, but the conversation quickly became professional. Not that Adele minded, she had loved her work, her career, and medical talk was home ground for her, and she silently recalled her happy nursing days. This clinic job was all right for the moment, but when Oliver was older she knew where her future lay.

Suddenly Gavin stood up. 'Adele—do forgive us, after saying I don't mix business with pleasure we then go on to discuss medical matters—most thoughtless, and I do apologise.'

Adele smiled. 'There's no need, really. It was a pleasure to listen. I want to keep in the swim of my profession, then it won't be so difficult to go back.'

'Ah—there speaks a woman who is ready to face the future.'

'It's a long way off yet.'

'But if you know what you want to do at a later date you can be paving the way now, and that brings me to a positive decision Matthew and I have come to—you're going to take me home while Matthew babysits.'

'I'm afraid I couldn't leave Oliver,' she said quickly.

'I bet he's asleep already,' Gavin suggested.

'Well—er—yes, but . . .'

'Get your coat then,' he commanded.

'Go off with Gavin and enjoy yourself, my dear,' Matthew agreed. 'I promise I'll look in on Oliver every half an hour. I shall enjoy a quiet time watching television. I have had a rather strenuous day.'

'I'm so sorry, Matthew, I didn't even ask if you enjoyed your golf?' Adele said, feeling that Matthew had been neglected.

'Excellent game, now I'm ready to relax.'

Adele had supposed Gavin would have walked home— cheek of the man, she thought, inviting himself to tea and then expecting a lift home. He helped her on with her velvet jacket, then slipped into his own blue quilted anorak.

'Keys?' he reminded her.

Adele's glance went to the hook in the hall and Gavin quickly forestalled her and took them down.

'Like to be chauffeur-driven for a change?' he asked with a smile.

Adele nodded. 'You know where you live,' she said flatly.

After putting Honey in the rear, he helped her in to the passenger seat, waiting while she did up the safety belt, then he got into the driving seat and after fiddling with the keys and the gear lever to get the feel of the car he backed out through the gates which Matthew had left open.

Adele was surprised at the distance he drove, then realised with horror that he was travelling on a country road that led well out of town. He didn't talk much as they went along which gave Adele time to develop her anger.

Eventually he turned off on a narrow lane, over a humpy bridge, and in the distance she could see coloured lights strung out beneath a thatched roof.

'*Bonne Bouché*, ever been here before?' he asked as he brought the car to a standstill on a gravel forecourt, then without giving her a chance to reply: 'No—you won't have, because it's only been opened a couple of months. *Bonne Bouché*,' he repeated. 'A choice morsel, in case your French is a bit rusty. It's a superb French establishment, restaurant and night club.'

'I thought I was taking you home,' she said tetchily.

'Matthew and I decided you needed a night out to enjoy yourself.'

'How do *you* know what I shall enjoy?' she answered huffily.

Gavin turned sharply to face her in the dark, only the reflection of the fairy lights illuminating the interior of her car.

'Stop it, Adele!' he snapped. 'I don't want to hear any more whining. So Life has been cruel—you've been through a tough time, but today out there on the hill I saw a brave young woman picking up the pieces ready to fight back. Trying to give Oliver a good time, but desperately struggling not to enjoy *her*self.'

'So what the hell has that got to do with you?' she retorted.

'Nothing—absolutely nothing—if I don't want it to, but tonight *I* want—I *want* to take you out to a meal, so, fair damsel, like it or lump it!' He unclicked his safety-belt, put the car keys in his pocket and opened his door. 'Coming?' he invited smoothly.

Adele's defiance made her clench her fists until her nails dug painfully into her palms.

'You,' she said, smarting with indignation, 'are—are—*hateful*!'

'Good,' he whispered softly, 'now we know exactly where we stand. But it still doesn't alter the fact that tonight I get what *I* want.'

Later, after he had ordered her out of the car, would, in

fact, have dragged her out if needs be, locked up, and with one hand maddeningly gentle under her elbow escorted her inside to a quiet alcove in subdued pink lighting, Adele silently fumed as she stared vacantly at the large elegant menu. She wondered helplessly just what he did want! Her eyes, dark with fury, skipped down the items on both pages but she read nothing, only ideas circulating in her brain of what he could want of her! The more she fought him the more he was going to demand, and how would that end? Oh, dear God, she prayed, how did I get myself into this? A gentle voice seemed to answer, and however hard she willed it away it came over loud and clear. You didn't—there's no way out. He wants to help you, be kind to you, and the voice died away.

Yes, she supposed that was all it was, just his way of forcing her to get out of her rut. Her anger began to subside, and she glanced up to meet his gaze assessing her as he so often did.

'Now read what the menu says and decide what you're going to eat,' he advised softly. 'Don't waste your energy trying to think of a way to get the keys and take off, leaving me stranded. Honey is devoted to me, she eats little girls like you for breakfast—well, you know how two bitches are together. Honey has only adoration for her master so I'm afraid she'll command the same respect from you.'

'Any respect I had for you—' she began, but was forced to turn her attention to the menu as the waiter came to their table.

The menu was useless. Gavin ordered for them both without asking her opinion. Steaks and vegetables, with melon for starters, and a bottle of French red wine, and when the waiter left Gavin leaned towards her.

'Any respect you had for me has now changed to contempt—right?' He waited, but Adele refused to argue. 'Matthew has been too soft with you, fair damsel. I'm sorry if you think I am being cruel, but it's time you started living again. You're not yet thirty, you have a whole lifetime before you.'

'I have Oliver,' Adele cut in sharply.

'Could we have just one hour without his name being mentioned? You're becoming the classic over-possessive mother, and you'll do him no good.'

The melon was brought and Adele was thankful that the service was so excellent. If Gavin Forbes kept on at her in this way she knew she would end up in tears, and she was determined not to give way again in front of him.

The Melon Surprise was delicious, cool and refreshing after the events of the day, and the steak which followed equally palatable. Gavin did not speak again as they ate, and Adele was aware of him occasionally lowering his gaze to his plate, but otherwise he kept his calculating eyes on her.

Eventually she sighed, and placed her knife and fork together beside a few vegetables she simply couldn't manage.

Gavin flicked his fingers towards her plate. 'Come on, there's a good girl, eat up.'

'I really couldn't, but thank you all the same. It was a lovely meal,' she admitted.

'Drink up your wine too. It's getting cold.'

At first she didn't realise he was teasing again, but when she comprehended his words she had to smile at him. He laughed heartily, a smooth brown laugh which had a seductive quality about it.

The waiter was quick to take away the plates, but not before Gavin had embarrassed Adele yet again.

'What penalty does the young lady have to pay for not clearing her plate, Claude?' he asked the waiter.

'Monsieur—ha—I think a fruit trifle must be eaten—with cream—and sherry—what you think, Monsieur Forbes?'

'Perfect, Claude, and you don't mind if I keep her here until she finishes this bottle of wine do you?'

'With such a charming guest, Monsieur—it will be our pleasure.'

He went away beaming hugely, pearly white teeth flashing provocatively.

Adele kept her gaze averted from Gavin's, but he raised

her chin with the handle end of his dessert spoon.

'Sad, brown velvet depths—honey-kissed eyes—rich creamy satin skin, high cheekbones now suffused with colour—a rare fair damsel,' he observed slowly.

'For goodness' sake,' Adele cried in agitation.

'Your husband was a lucky man, darling.'

'And *I* was extremely fortunate,' she answered in exasperation.

For once she had the last word as the waiter brought huge dairy cream-topped sherry trifles, and coffee. But Gavin being Gavin was not a man to allow a woman to have the last word.

'You were both blessed with a rare quality, for such perfect marriages are hard to find,' he said with sincerity.

Adele surveyed the trifle cautiously before she said: 'I don't think I said our marriage was perfect—few are that, I agree. Perhaps we don't really value what we have until it's gone. I only know, Dr Forbes, that the emptiness I'm left with is indescribable, but I'm also sensible enough to acknowledge that I have to start building a new life. It's kind of everyone to want to help, but I do have to try to work things out on my own.'

Gavin reached across the table and placed his hand firmly over hers. She tried to pull away, but he kept her fingers trapped beneath his long, slender ones, his eyes shining, and reflecting his admiration of her, as he gazed long and lovingly into her eyes.

'The fairest damsel in all the world,' he whispered.

Adele managed to pull her hand free and she tackled the sherry trifle but not from enthusiasm, more with hate.

There was a lull in the conversation, and then Gavin began to talk about Adele's forthcoming tests and consultation. Perhaps at last he realised he had tried her patience to the limit. He asked about her family, remembering the little she had told him when she had first met him at her interview. For the moment at least a truce seemed to have been declared. She poured the cream over her coffee spoon and watched it swirl round on the top of the cup, trying not to think of Oliver, and his reaction if he should waken and find only Matthew at home. Poor Matthew. She doubted that he had anticipated such a dull evening, and she felt convinced that he hadn't really approved of Gavin taking her off.

She tried discreetly to look at her watch.

'Quite early really,' a masculine voice agreed with what she had already discovered. 'That's why there are so few people here—it will be full by nine o'clock. You see—eating a good meal was quite painless wasn't it? When did you last cook a three-course meal for yourelf and Oliver?'

'I do cook each day—honestly—although I don't expect you to believe me. Naturally I tend to prepare what I know Oliver prefers.'

'Of course I believe you, Adele. If Oliver wasn't getting a nutritious diet he wouldn't look so sturdy. He's a fine lad.' He sighed. 'He just needs—um—shall we say a little healthy competition?'

'What do you mean?'

Gavin held up his hands in despair. 'See—you've got me at it now—no Oliver talk I said.'

'That hour was up long since,' she quipped with a smile.

'Just as you are in danger of becoming over-possessive with Oliver, there's a great danger of allowing him to become obsessed with concern for you.'

'A four year old?' Adele's doubt showed in her frown.

'The formative years—remember?' Gavin brought the topic of conversation to a close by calling the waiter for the bill.

Adele stood up. 'I'd better go to the Ladies room—but—I have no handbag, no money, nothing,' she said in mock reproach.

'You don't need anything—do you?' A momentary look of concern came over his face, and Adele felt pleased that for once she had almost caught him napping. She dug her hands in her pockets. 'I'm not suitably dressed to be taken out to dinner,' she said. 'I do prefer to be prepared.'

Gavin stood up, looking her up and down. 'It was the dress which gave me the idea—after all, I'm not exactly dressed for dinner either—thank goodness in these days conventions are more relaxed.'

Adele saw the appropriate sign and briefly left Gavin.
When she returned he was at the desk talking to the
manager and a moment or two later they were outside, but
not at the front entrance by which they had entered, but at
the rear where the sound of rushing water reached Adele's
ears.

'Just a little walk to aid your digestion—*our* digestion,'
he laughed, and grasped her hand in his as he guided her
down some steps to a narrow path which led through a
fairy-lit wood and out by a floodlit weir.

'We'll bring Oliver one day,' Gavin said lightly. 'He'd
love it here.' His tone changed. 'About Matthew,' he said
sharply, the usual light-heartedness gone out of his voice.

'What about Matthew?' Adele enquired.

'That's what I want *you* to tell *me*.'

'I don't understand you,' Adele said, puzzled.

Gavin stopped on the deserted pathway and pulled her
round to face him.

Without realising it she was becoming accustomed to his
constant scrutiny of her and she faced him fearlessly in the
half-gloom.

'What is Matthew to you? What are you to him?' he
demanded.

Adele felt her body go tense. Hadn't she questioned this
self-same situation?

'He's an old colleague, first,' she said quietly, 'secondly a
very dear friend who treated and did his utmost for Bernie's
widowed mother, and then Bernie.'

'There's nothing between you?—not even a kiss?—and
what about the cuddles Oliver mentioned?'

This was absurd. What was the matter with the man—he
couldn't be jealous! He was already committed to that
other woman!

'Oliver sees Matthew as a very kind uncle, who has been
considerate and helpful to both of us.'

'Nothing more?' Gavin repeated in disbelief.

'Why the inquisition?' Adele replied impatiently. 'No,
there *is* nothing more.'

'Then, fair damsel, Matthew won't mind if I take a few liberties.'

She was enclosed in his arms before she had time to protest, enclosed in such a way that there was no escape. His sensuous mouth, warm and exciting, trapped hers against his, so that however unyielding, she was forced to respond. She closed her eyes desperately pleading for release but his mouth was in full command of hers, and he knew how to make her submit. Her struggles were useless, his hands seeking out sensitive areas of her slim body as he pressed her against him.

When he let her go she was too exhausted to speak except to whisper croakily: 'You beast! Is nothing sacred to you?'

'You're a woman, Adele. Whatever has been before is now over and I simply had to make you remember why you are a woman.'

'You're despicable,' she said angrily, apprehensive of reminding him of his loyalties.

'I'm sorry you think that, darling. It's no crime to have feelings of passion—if your marriage was that good then you'll want to experience more of the same. When you're ready, when you fully appreciate that *your* life has to go on you'll see it as a compliment to your first marriage to love a second time. Of course I don't want to force my attentions on you—but, think for a moment, Adele, isn't there a pulse vibrating passionately somewhere inside you? Isn't it good to feel that glimmer of excited anticipation?'

'No—it's cheap and ugly,' she growled back at him.

'Don't fight me, Adele,' he whispered, as once more he hugged her in his arms until she was breathless, one hand exploring, caressing, arousing in her every nerve of desire. 'You are a woman made to love, to love and be loved,' he went on. 'It isn't right to suppress sexual desire, Adele. All your vibrant youth is screaming to be unleashed. Don't you feel just a wee bit excited? Aren't you trembling with passion?' he breathed.

'With anger, and shame,' she yelled at him before his lips crushed against her open mouth, filling her with fiery ecstasy, and the pain which rebellion brought.

More clients leaving the restaurant could be heard approaching with banter and laughter, but this did not deter Gavin Frobes. He merely guided Adele backwards between some shrubs, his demanding kisses an unleashing of his own craving.

Breathlessly he broke apart, still holding her while he recovered from the anguish he had instilled upon himself.

'Adele,' he moaned, and pressed his face into her neck and she felt his fingers digging into her shoulders as he fought for control.

Adele did not know whether to feel pity for him or be afraid, but emotion was running so intense between them that slow tears spilled from her eyes and ran down her cheeks.

After several minutes Gavin straightened, and pulled a handkerchief from his pocket, gently wiping her tear-stained face.

'I can't take you home like this,' he said softly.

'I was supposed to be taking you home,' she reminded him gently, dreading the thought of ever coming face to face with his lady friend again.

In the dim lighting she knew he was smiling down at her. She couldn't be sure what he had intended to revive in her but she felt certain that he had succeeded only in torturing himself.

He placed an arm round her and slowly they walked the circular route back to the forecourt.

Honey was whining to get out.

'No, Honey, we shall soon be home—good girl,' he soothed, and as if conversation was exhausted he drove away without speaking.

Adele noticed that it was about nine-thirty as they passed a church clock in the suburb bordering the one in which she lived. Gavin pulled in to the picturesque grounds of an elegant three-storey block of luxury flats.

He looked across at Adele and smiled, a genuinely warm smile in which there was no hint of torment.

'Come and meet Mother,' he invited.

'You live with your mother?' she asked, surprised.

'No, she's staying with me for a few days. She's been out with friends today, but there's a light on so she is home.'

'I really ought to get back.'

'It's still early, Adele—please, just a cup of coffee—it would please Mother.'

'Just a quick one then.'

Why did she fall in with his suggestions so meekly? His warmth had surprised her, reminding her again of his changing moods. He had said he didn't mix business with pleasure, yet he had eagerly shown his affection for the tall, raven-haired woman during business hours at the clinic. Did she know how capricious Gavin Forbes was? There was no other word for it. Adele had been so certain of his relationship with this other woman yet he had shown no restraint in his thirst for making love to Adele. It aroused a curiousness within her. His mother, his home—the who, why and where of his sophisticated companion! She got out of the car and smoothed down her dress while Gavin opened the hatchback to let Honey out.

Gavin gave Adele the keys.

'Perhaps you'd better lock the car doors while I just take Honey to the garden at the back.'

She watched him running off with Honey barking and jumping at his side.

Gavin Forbes was an odd character. At first she had considered him unfeeling at the clinic, but now she knew he was capable of a deep and exciting passion. She wasn't sure what he had aroused in her, but at this moment she did find herself wondering what his mother would be like. She would be elderly, grey, tall and dignified she expected—after all, Gavin was probably thirty-five or even more, his hair being of a rich colour and his face clear and fresh keeping him youthful-looking.

Her thoughts were interrupted as Honey came eagerly up to her with Gavin in close pursuit.

'Still here? Good—but that surprises me,' he said with a chuckle. 'Having given you the opportunity to escape I rather thought you'd seize it.'

'That would have been rude. At least give me credit for

good manners, Dr Forbes. It was kind of you to take me out to dinner, thank you, and for the time and patience with Oliver this afternoon.'

'I doubt that I can compete with his father, but it gave me pleasure to keep you both company, Adele—now, let's go inside.'

She accompanied him into the entrance hall where they waited for the lift which quickly took them up to the top floor.

A few steps along a carpeted passageway and Gavin opened the door of number fifteen. Everywhere was light, with oatmeal carpeting and pale tangerine walls and from the inviting square hall Gavin took her into the lounge. It was a huge L-shaped room with enormous windows hidden behind oyster-coloured velvet drapes.

'Hullo, Mother, you got back safely then?' Gavin greeted. 'I've brought Adele to meet you.'

A woman rose from the chair and switched off the television before turning towards them.

'Oh please don't let me interrupt your viewing,' Adele said, but she was glad of the chance to study Gavin's mother as she walked sedately across the room. She was petite and much younger than Adele had anticipated.

'Ah, Gavin, and Mrs Kinsey I believe.' She held out her beringed hand and shook Adele's warmly.

'How do you do, Mrs—'

'Mrs Lascelles,' Gavin put in quickly. 'Mother remarried after my father died,' he explained.

'So you are the delightful new recruit to our clinic,' Mrs Lascelles said, and Adele detected a faint French accent. 'I've heard all about you—come, sit with me, *chérie*, and we shall talk woman to woman. Gavin, the coffee should be just about ready. I put in on the stove when you telephoned.'

Adele half turned and Gavin gave her a saucy wink.

'All part of the plot. I rang Mother when you were otherwise engaged.' He disappeared and Mrs Lascelles guided Adele to a luxurious settee while she sat opposite in a high-backed rocker.

'Tell me, *chérie*, how have you enjoyed the visit to *Bonne Bouché*?'

'Very much, thank you,' Adele replied but a trifle shyly while she still assessed the older woman. She found herself desperately tied up with her inadequate mental arithmetic. If Gavin were about thirty-five years of age his mother must be approaching sixty, but she was so youthful in appearance and sprightly in step.

'I know how 'ard it ees for you, Adele. You may think that because my 'usband, Gavin's father, died many years ago I forget—but—' she shook her head decisively. 'Not so—not so—I think often of the short but 'appy time we spent together.'

Adele smiled, and Gavin came through the door pushing a tea-trolley. He poured coffee from a tall pottery coffee pot.

'I really shouldn't you know. I've had more than enough already,' Adele said, but took the matching pottery cup and saucer, admiring the natural shade of the pottery with its superb design of poppies, and field mice climbing up the corn.

Gavin came to sit beside her after he had poured coffee for his mother and himself.

'You would like a sandwich perhaps, or a biscuit?' Mrs Lascelles offered.

'I considered trying to tempt her,' Gavin cut in, 'as you can see she doesn't look after herself properly, however she has eaten quite well this evening.'

He smiled across at her generously, and Adele saw that mother and son were alike in colouring and in this ageless appearance.

'I was telling Adele that although the years have passed, I do not forget, and I understand the stress of what she is going through.'

'As I told you on the telephone, Mother, I met Adele and her young son, Oliver up on the hill, trying to fly a kite.'

'And how old is Oliver?' his mother asked.

'Just four.'

'Ah—Gavin was just a leetle older—almost six years.'

'Then you don't remember your father?' Adele turned to Gavin, trying to steer the conversation away from herself and Oliver.

'Hardly—I have a picture in my mind, mainly stimulated I expect from photographs.'

'Ours was a much stranger marriage than yours I expect,' Mrs Lascelles said. 'We met and married in the early days of the war in France. Gavin's father was an English pilot, shot down near our village. I had just begun to 'elp at the 'ospital so we patched him up and then took him into the hills to hide. I took him food—being always petite I could disguise myself as a schoolgirl, so pedalling along on my bicycle the Germans were not suspicious.'

'They must have been frightening times for you,' Adele said, intrigued by the story.

Mrs Lascelles shrugged. 'Oh yes—but we had only one thought—to thwart the enemy. Taking food daily to my 'andsome English officer we quickly fell in love and when things got bad we moved 'im to the convent in the mountains, and there we were married in secret. I and my family were involved in many underground activities, and eventually when I became pregnant they helped us escape to England. Zat is why Gavin is so Eenglish.'

'You never returned to France?' Adele asked, sipping her delicious coffee, but interested as Mrs Lascelles reminisced.

'Yes, but many years later. After Guy, who survived the war, died of polio in 1949 I could not come to terms with my grief. I lived only for Gavin, and knew that his father wished him to be English so I did not return to France until much later. It was 'ard, but I made my life here in England. Guy's family were kind to me but they could not understand why *their* son should fall in love and marry a French girl and if I had not had Gavin they would surely have sent me back to France.'

'If I may be personal, Mrs Lascelles, you look so young now. It doesn't seem possible that you could have been married during the war.'

Gavin and his mother laughed.

'Eternal youth, *ma chérie*,' Mrs Lascelles said happily.

'You married again?' Adele pursued gently.

'Not until I was over forty years old. Now, I want to tell you, Adele, don't wait that long. I was 'appy with Guy's family. Because of Gavin who was a charming little boy I stayed with the Forbes family. They were wealthy, and could educate Gavin better than I could have done alone, but I know now that I should have married again much sooner. Gavin was used to the older people—he should have had a normal family home and it was not that I did not have the opportunities.' She leaned across and patted Adele's knee. 'Your grief will become easier, *ma chérie*, somesing that you will keep inside you, grief will change into cherished memories that you will never forget, but on the outside—for your son's sake, the world must be a 'appy place. You are young and pretty—you will not be alone for long, Adele.'

Tears pricked at the back of Adele's eyes. She appreciated that Gavin's mother's words were well-meaning, but no one could understand *her* personal feelings. She didn't want anyone to take Bernie's place, not in her life, or Oliver's. But that night after she'd driven home, and Matthew had left, she went to bed realising that in Oliver's memory already Bernie was something to be remembered, but without the importance that the present held. For Oliver it was today and tomorrow which mattered, and even deep inside herself Adele felt a stirring towards a different kind of tomorrow.

CHAPTER FIVE

THE weekend had been so full of activity that Monday morning arrived with renewed anxiety for Adele. She reproached herself for being taken off by Gavin Forbes when she should have spent time with Oliver, preparing him to return to nursery school. He was full of exuberance when he woke and greeted Adele with the fact that he liked 'him', and when could 'him' come to tea again.

'Dr Forbes is a very busy man, darling,' she explained. 'I don't expect I shall see much of him at the clinic today.'

Oliver thought about this carefully while Adele chivvied him into getting dressed, and she could sense that he was remembering that he had to go to nursery school.

When they reached the gate he started to cry and was almost hysterical by the time Mrs Dawkins managed to extract him from Adele.

Sheila could see at a glance that something was wrong when Adele arrived at the clinic.

'Sit down, Adele, a cup of coffee will revive you. This second week will probably seem worse than the first, but in a month's time you'll be laughing about it.'

'I doubt that,' Adele muttered. 'I should have stuck to my guns and left on Friday.'

'That's wishful thinking, Adele,' a stern voice said behind her. 'I told you I wouldn't accept your resignation and if needs be I'd have come and dragged you here.'

'Your arrogance doesn't impress me, Dr Forbes.' Adele released her pent-up nerves in a fit of anger. 'I've been too easily led by other people. I'm only concerned about Oliver, and he needs me,' she said adamantly.

'He needs to be treated sensibly, Adele.' Gavin made a sign to Sheila to leave them, and he faced Adele with haughty contempt in his green eyes. She had dared to call

78

him arrogant, and in front of another member of the staff. He wouldn't like that. 'I presume you've had trouble with Oliver this morning—well, what did you expect after a pleasant weekend at home with a doting mother?'

'I'm *not* a doting mother,' Adele replied, her cheeks aflame with anger. 'I *care* about my son which is more than some mothers do. I don't *have* to work.'

'That is where you are wrong,' Gavin said slowly. 'The way you are behaving this morning is living proof that you need to be separated from Oliver frequently.'

'Well I'm not going to be, for you or for anyone else,' she replied flatly.

'Stop behaving stroppily, Adele. Drink your coffee and consider your clients. As I've already explained to you it will take Oliver two weeks to get used to his new way of life, and then you'll be amazed at the change in him. Give the lad a break and stop smothering him—you'll only succeed in making a baby of him, and he won't thank you for that.'

He swung round on his heel and went off in search of Sheila.

The other girls arrived and were sympathetic, but Dr Forbes was taking the first consultation and asked Adele to bring coffee to the consulting room before his first patient arrived. She expected another lecture, but he was reading the patient's questionnaire and didn't bother to look up let alone thank her for the coffee.

Despite her worry Adele concentrated on her work and the morning passed quickly and when she met Oliver she was dismayed to find him pale and subdued.

'Don't worry, Mrs Kinsey. The second week is usually more traumatic than the first. He's been quite happy, though quiet,' Mrs Dawkins assured her.

It pained Adele to see him so miserable, for that was how she interpreted his silence, and after the happy weekend it all seemed such needless aggravation.

He cried bitterly on the following two mornings which meant that when Adele was required to be the patient instead of nurse her blood pressure was somewhat high. Gavin Forbes's colleague was a much older man, nearing retirement age, Adele decided, but so understanding, and kind, that her fears were quickly allayed and he listened patiently to her explanations of Oliver. Sitting opposite him, watching him go through the questionnaire she had so impatiently filled up, made her wish she had taken a little more care with her answers. He was sympathetic in the loss of her husband, and afterwards Adele realised that most of his advice was the same as that given by Matthew and Gavin Forbes, but offered with profound sincerity.

Adele noticed that the visiting doctor made straight for Dr Forbes's office after her consultation was over and she imagined how her employer would love telling his colleague what an over-possessive mother she was. It didn't much matter what they thought, she consoled herself, she still harboured the intention of leaving the clinic eventually, and then she would quickly be forgotten. Dr Forbes would probably be very gratified if she left. She suspected that he considered her home commitments distracted her from giving of her best in her work.

For the remainder of the morning she chased up clients' results, completing their files in readiness to go to the various doctors who compiled the final report. She missed taking patients round on the tests, but found that she had time to reflect over the changes which this job had incurred. She smiled secretly to herself when she recalled the Sunday afternoon and evening spent in Gavin's company. She had to admit that his attention had brought a certain stimulant to her emotions, although she was sure such an event was never likely to happen again. Deep down she thought him fickle, so no wonder his lady friend insisted on part-time married nurses as employees, so that personal involvements were less likely.

He was right about one thing. He wasn't guilty of mixing business with pleasure. He mostly treated Adele with the same terseness of manner he had shown on her very first day, leaving her mystified as to his behaviour towards her during their evening out. A one-off interlude of romantic persuasion, she supposed. Testing her out, reminding her of hidden desires, perhaps his way of reawakening her to the need of some social life. She could well do without such reminders.

One morning the following week when she reached the clinic she hardly had time to remove her coat when the intercom buzzed. Sheila answered, then with a slightly curious look said: 'Adele—Dr Forbes would like to see you in his office.'

Adele's heart sank. The request was unusual as well as unexpected. Then she remembered her own screening recently. What had they found? Something awful to be this quick—something which needed instant treatment? There couldn't be anything wrong with her, there mustn't be— what would happen to Oliver?

Her heart was pounding frantically as she knocked on the office door and entered in reply to his 'Come in'.

She walked briskly up to his desk, tension mounting, agitated with impatience when with grim consternation he carried on examining some paperwork. God, she thought, it must be bad news, so bad that he couldn't bring himself to tell her. Then he tossed a bundle of papers towards her, thrusting a folder into her hands.

'For heaven's sake, Adele, you've been here long enough to know that I don't prepare a report until I have *all* the test results.'

Adele felt the blood drain away from her cheeks. In fact it felt as if it were simply draining away from her body altogether. She went quite limp and just stared blankly at the man sitting at the desk.

Gavin Forbes leaned forward, peering into her face. 'Whatever's the matter?' he asked, his tone much gentler.

She half grunted as she began to pick up the floating pieces of paper. 'I'm sorry,' she muttered.

'Adele—what is it?'

She dared to meet his concerned expression with her own vacant stare. The relief made her legs turn to jelly.

'I . . . I imagined you'd sent for me because—'

'Because what?' Gavin demanded.

Adele shook her head as if shaking herself out of some

sort of stupor. 'My screening—I stupidly imagined—they'd
found something—awful.' Her voice became slower, and
lower so that the final word was barely audible.

Gavin placed his hand containing his pen down on the
desk with a decisive thud, then stood up and walked to the
window, hands sliding up and down his thighs. Adele heard
his footsteps pacing the floor behind her.

'Stupid—right,' he agreed angrily. 'Imagined—you imagined—well stop imagining that everything bad happens
to you. There are others in the world besides you, and your
job is to allay their fears, help to put their minds at rest and
my job is to do the same by means of compiling a report—a
report for which I need all the relevant information.' He
was shouting now and although Adele was scanning
through the papers she had retrieved she was trembling too
much to see what she had done wrong.

'I'm sorry about this,' she managed in a more coherent
voice.

'Stop saying you're sorry,' he yelled. 'Being sorry doesn't
put it right. Go away and get it right.'

He returned to the desk and gave her not one set of
clients' notes, but several.

'I'm sure you have nothing to worry about concerning
your own screening, Adele. You are one of my staff,
therefore your report will be compiled by Dr Hill-Stevens
and sent to your home direct, a copy to your own GP. You
are really no good to me, Adele, unless you can forget your
personal circumstances, and concentrate on your work.'

'When would you like me to leave?' she enquired sarcas-
tically, a renewed flow of blood to her brain causing her to
react smartly.

'Who said anything about leaving? You need this job—
more than you realise. I don't expect you to learn everything in five minutes, but you do have to consider your
clients first. I was telling Matthew how well you had
acquainted yourself with the work. I'm disappointed in
you, Adele, not because of this minor oversight in seeing
that everything I need is in the file, but I had hoped you
were indulging less in self-pity now that Oliver has settled

down. I was wrong—you're still bringing Beecroft to work with you. You've been here over two weeks now, it's high time you had learned to leave personal matters outside the door.'

'If you had expected me to do that, Dr Forbes, then you shouldn't have engaged me, knowing the circumstances,' she argued hotly.

'I engaged you, Adele, because Matthew wanted me to and for the very reasons you've just admitted. I'm sure you don't want to let Matthew down.'

He was insufferable, there was just no reasoning with him, and as she tried to contain the pile of notes in her arms everything seemed to sway. She grabbed the edge of the desk to steady herself then walked slowly out of his room.

She went along to the general office where the files were kept, and spread all the untidy papers out on a table so that she could start again. It took her some time to sift them into the correct order and while she was still working on them Sheila came in.

'Ah—there you are, something wrong?' the senior nurse asked.

'According to Dr Forbes something is missing from these files, but as far as I can see all the results are here. You wouldn't have a minute to check I suppose, Sheila?' Adele pleaded.

'Sure—let's see—' She checked through each client's file. 'Yes, everything is to hand, but—the boss does have his little whims, and I expect I forgot to emphasise the fact that he likes the results in a certain order—the radiologist's report first, followed by mammogram for women clients, then the electro-cardiogram, etcetera.'

Sheila went on to explain the exact order of preference Dr Forbes insisted upon, and soon the notes were all tidily back in the files.

'I expect you think he's just being petty, but it is easier for the doctors to complete the report sheet more quickly and accurately if we all work to the same system. Take them back, Adele, make your peace with Sir,' she quipped with a grin.

'I'd like to throw them back at him the way he did at me,' Adele said vindictively.

'Then he'd only humiliate you by making you sort them all out again, and he'd probably stand over you while you did it.' Sheila laughed. 'All bosses try your patience to the limit at times, but he does have one or two things on his mind at present,' she excused.

Adele felt ready to explode—and after all he'd just preached at her about leaving personal problems at the door! Well here was one person who would not pander to his petty administrations, she would let him see what she thought of his over-officious nit-pickings, and see if she cared a hoot about getting the sack.

Adele knocked on his office door without attempting to contain her ever-increasing annoyance, and went in without waiting for the invitation. Gavin looked mildly surprised, but she didn't give him time to comment as she marched boldly up to his desk and plonked the pile of folders in front of him with a loud thud.

'*All* the test results were there, Dr Forbes, if you had just taken the trouble to look for them,' she said petulantly.

She had reached the door, congratulating herself on at least giving as good as she got when he called her back.

'Come back, Adele,' he said in a surprisingly seductive voice.

She returned hesitantly, wishing she hadn't been quite so courageous for now she felt anything but brave as she stood before him while he observed her with those ice-clear eyes.

'I'm not used to employing rebellious staff, Adele—will you kindly remove those files to the side desk so that I can continue to do my work.'

'You told me to go and get it right—this I have done and if I move the files again things are liable to get misplaced—Sir.'

'Don't be impertinent, Adele. I realise you're a little over-wrought as you were obviously expecting the worse from your screening—you are also insinuating, I think, that I am making a fuss over nothing in reference to the files—

perhaps you even think I rearranged the paperwork in order to have a go at you?'

'You might well do that if you want to needle me sufficiently into leaving,' she retorted brazenly.

He got up rather suddenly, and before she had time to think, was round to her side of the desk.

'Not one more word about leaving, my girl,' he said savagely, his face levelling with her, his lips so smooth and well-shaped, tantalisingly close to hers. 'You demonstrate this doleful lament because I presume you think circumstances behove you to do so, but you can't fool me, Adele, beneath it all you're just as much of a temptress as any other woman.'

'I have given you no cause to say such a thing,' she cried outraged.

Gavin gripped her shoulders firmly giving her a slight shake.

'Just remember one thing, Adele, I do *not* mix business with pleasure—but beware—I like to settle scores. It seems such a shame not to take the bait when it's so freely offered, but I have my principles. Just as well, or you would not be leaving my office looking so neat and trim.'

After raking over her contemptuously he nodded meaningfully towards the pile of folders, and as she moved them, sighing deeply, he added: 'Now get out of my office and don't come in again uninvited.'

Adele went quickly to the ladies room in order to let her flushed cheeks cool down. Damn, damn, damn, she cursed to herself, letting off steam, he was the one who continually baited her, but cool, clever swine that he was he could so effectively turn the tables and make it seem that she was the provocative one. It was incredible how in the short time she had worked at *A Votre Santé* clinic this wretched man could extract a wild, insurgent streak she didn't know she possessed.

By mid-morning the early session of screenings had ended and after coffee the next clients began to arrive. It was Adele's job to tidy the consulting rooms, and to be in attendance during breast, abdominal and pelvic examinations on women clients which were carried out by a doctor as well as cervical smears. As she was tidying the coffee things away Dr Forbes came up behind her.

'You can bring Mrs Tucker through, Adele. I shall need you then in about half an hour's time when I carry out my examination. I trust you won't run off anywhere in the meantime.' He turned so that his thigh brushed hers, almost clung intimately to her side for one breath-taking moment, so that she glanced quickly at him. Such contacts were courting disaster she knew. His eyes were that soft shade of turquoise again, gently wooing, seducing her and she knew that she very definitely ought to leave the clinic, but oh how much she wanted to stay!

Dr Gavin Forbes was at his most bewitching and competent during his consultations. The pleasantries he exchanged with Mrs Tucker put her entirely at her ease so that she broke into hysterical laughter when he began to tap various parts of her body for reflex action.

'I'm sorry to giggle like a schoolgirl,' she apologised, unable to contain her amusement any longer. 'I feel like a xylophone being played.'

'That's nothing to what I'm going to do to you in a minute,' Gavin warned his client before he ran the end of the instrument he was using up the soles of her feet. It elicited a shriek, as was to be expected in normal healthy clients, and all three laughed heartily, any last barriers of nervous anticipation removed.

He cast a sidelong glance at Adele when he had taken a cervical smear, indicating that she could now take the sterile trolley away and prepare the samples for analysis at the special laboratory. All signs of familiarity with her had vanished.

Adele felt almost sorry when the weekend arrived, although she was pleased for Oliver's sake, but thankfully the following week saw a big improvement in her son's general attitude. He chattered eagerly, and mostly about nursery school. Adele hated having to admit that the great Dr Forbes had been right, but all her worries and concern for Oliver gradually melted away. She was able to give her whole-hearted interest to her work, she loved meeting clients, she enjoyed the harmonious working relationships with her colleagues, and when weekends came round she missed their company. Above all, no matter how much Gavin Forbes despised her, even ignored her unless duty demanded some liaison, she couldn't help but admire him. She knew he had been right to brow-beat her into taking up the threads of life again, and Matthew had been so clever in recognising that the owner of *A Votre Santé* clinic was the right man to relate to Adele's needs.

It was a Saturday morning a week or so later while she was enjoying a leisurely breakfast with Oliver when the ominous buff envelope marked 'Private and Confidential' arrived.

Oliver was eager to go off to play which gave Adele time to read the full report Dr Hill-Stevens had made from her screening and test results. She sighed with relief when she learned that there was nothing more wrong with her than a low blood count which would explain her feeling of inadequacy, tiredness, and a tendency to weeping as well as occasional dizziness, all of which would be speedily remedied by means of a course of iron tablets. No doubt Gavin Forbes would relish the chance to say 'told you so', but on the other hand he was more likely to ignore the whole issue. In retrospect she saw the events of that Sunday as incidental. Evidently Gavin had the day to himself and the chance meeting up on the hill had presented an opportunity for light relief to him. He had been kind to Oliver, charming to herself for no other reason than pity. The trouble was, Adele reflected, the incident had disturbed her more than she liked to admit.

No one at the clinic ever talked about the private life of Dr Forbes and Adele was too discreet to make enquiries, or was it that she didn't really want to know? She could ruminate over those few eventful hours, indulge in some speculation as to what might have been if it weren't for that tall, curvaceous woman who had visited the clinic. Was Adele day-dreaming or had that suggestive 'darling' been his companion's way of saying 'hands off'?

He wasn't actually married, Adele affirmed, not legally, never mind about their common-law status, so he was at liberty to pull any woman he chose! She shrugged such thoughts off with disgust, and busied herself with the household tasks.

Matthew spent the evening with them, and discussed at length the entire report with Adele after Oliver had gone to bed.

'A similar report will have reached your own doctor by now, so make an early appointment and get started on a course of iron as soon as possible, my dear. It will make all the difference—now is the time to look after yourself. Oliver has settled down happily and you're enjoying your work at the clinic, so pamper yourself a bit,' Matthew advised her.

Sunday morning was another dull day, dark and dreary, reminding Adele on this day when British summer time officially ended that winter was approaching.

Oliver slept late so the whole day seemed mixed up, but after an even later than usual lunch they dressed up in warm coats and went round the garden, between them picking the last of the bedraggled dahlias, and some of the huge chrysanths to take to the crematorium.

Adele would have gone every week, she had in fact for the first two months until Matthew had gently reproached her, suggesting that it was a morbid habit for a child to cope with, so she had accepted his suggestion of going about once a month.

These days there was less time for grief and self-pity. During a spell of bad weather it had been necessary to get the swimming pool emptied and covered for the winter, and at Matthew's suggestion she had started to put her car in the garage beside Bernie's. She still couldn't bring herself to do anything about the Volvo. She knew it would deteriorate standing idle, and occasionally she would sit in it and let the engine tick smoothly over, but she couldn't bear to part with it, nor to imagine anyone else sitting in Bernie's seat.

The rain had eased to a fine drizzle, so with her armful of

flowers in the rear of her car she opened the gates and the garage door and reversed out into the driveway.

'I may as well leave the garage door open. It's too nasty to stay out long, Oliver,' she said.

She had almost reached the open gateway when the front of a car swept in and blocked her way.

Adele braked hard and muttered under her breath as she recognised Gavin Forbes sitting behind the wheel of a superior Daimler.

Oliver knelt up on the seat and shrieked with delight.

'It's Honey—and him,' he cried excitedly.

An impatient blast on his horn told Adele that he expected to be allowed in, so reluctantly she changed gear and drove forward again with the Daimler only inches away from her bumper.

Serve him right if I slammed on my brakes, she thought defiantly, as in the mirror she could see him grinning boyishly as he drove bumper to bumper forcing her back to the garage.

Gavin got out of his car and reached Adele's window before she could unleash her safety belt.

'Not going to the hill today, surely?' he asked, pushing his hand over Adele's shoulder to ruffle Oliver's hair.

Adele was in danger of being suffocated.

'I think I'd better move,' she said and as she got out she explained: 'We were going to the crematorium with some flowers.'

'Then I won't delay you, or intrude, perhaps some other time, though I did want to talk to you.'

'Oh?' Adele prepared herself for more of Gavin Forbes's decrees. It seemed to her that all doctors were alike on that score, for, she remembered, she would never have met Gavin Forbes, or even heard of his *A Votre Santé* clinic if Matthew had not decreed that she should send Oliver to nursery school so that she could work and have a new interest.

Oliver squeezed himself out from behind Adele's seat and in seconds Gavin was swinging him round wildly, wellies and all.

'Oh, do mind your suit, Gavin,' she said with concern, 'Oliver's all muddy.'

She felt her cheeks flooding with colour at the easy way she had used his Christian name. She had deliberately endeavoured not to do this, even though he had tried to torment her into doing so. He was, after all, her employer, and if she started to use his name informally then she might forget at the clinic. She couldn't imagine ever being on such familiar terms with him, but hadn't she just proved how easy it was to be persuaded?

Gavin openly laughed at her embarrassment.

'Well done, fair damsel, I thought you were never going to get around to it,' he said.

'Mummy, let's go to the hill?' Oliver pleaded earnestly.

'Not today, darling, it isn't nice enough, besides there's no wind.'

Oliver held Gavin's hand tightly. 'I . . . I want him to come to our house again. I . . . I haven't got anyone else to play with—Mummy—please?'

Adele couldn't help laughing, and Gavin too, but she intended to be firm.

'Perhaps another time,' she said.

Oliver's smiles changed quickly to a frown, his bottom lip trembling.

'Another time, Oliver, as Mummy says,' Gavin agreed. 'Unless—were you only going to the crematorium and then home again?'

'Yes,' Adele affirmed.

'Then why not let me drive you up there? I won't intrude on your private pilgrimage and then how about having tea with me today? My mother would love to meet Oliver.'

Adele fell silent. How could she refuse without seeming to be rude? She wanted desperately to enjoy Gavin's company, but she was afraid. Afraid of her own emotions as well as hearing things about Gavin's private life which she would prefer not to know.

'Is Matthew coming this evening?' Gavin asked.

'No, he telephoned yesterday. He had to attend a seminar at the hospital this morning so he was hoping to play golf this afternoon.'

'I saw him at the seminar myself. I also saw your GP, Ingrid Sewell, and we talked about you.'

Adele raised her eyebrows.

'As you'll have read on your report, and as I suspected, you're anaemic, so to save you an immediate visit to Ingrid I got a prescription from her for you. Here are the pills—take them regularly and keep them out of Oliver's reach. They are not sweets, Oliver, but something to make Mummy a bit more lively. Will you remind her to take one every morning?'

'She's had those before,' Oliver said.

Gavin handed them over to Adele.

'How thoughtful of you,' she said, secretly wishing he would allow her to deal with such things herself.

'Make an appointment and go along to see Ingrid in about a week or ten days time. Take Oliver too. Now, shall we get going?'

'I—I ought to bring my car, otherwise it means bringing you out later on,' Adele said.

'Put your car away—you were kind enough to ferry me around the other week.'

Already Oliver was pulling Gavin towards the dark chocolate-coloured Daimler, but Gavin stood his ground, waiting to help Adele with the garage door, and when it was all locked up they set off.

When they reached the crematorium Adele felt obliged to suggest that Gavin went with them to the Garden of Memory.

'No, Adele, I'll wait here,' he said softly. 'I understand that this is a private shrine and you need a few moments alone. No, Oliver,' he insisted as Oliver began to cling to him, 'you go and help Mummy with those lovely flowers while I turn the car round.'

Oliver immediately transferred his hand to Adele's and walked sedately by her side as they went to the part of the garden where a plaque to Bernie's memory was fixed to the wall. Just beneath it was a large stone vase and Adele threw the old flowers out and arranged her colourful bouquet in their place.

Oliver chattered all the time he was helping her, but Adele stood back a pace or two in silent reverence. Dear Bernie, she pleaded, help me to do what is right for Oliver. Help me to bear the loneliness—oh, darling, I miss you so very much. The tears pricked at the back of her eyes as they always did when she remembered Bernie, not as the handsome, debonair young man she had married, but the pale, emaciated figure who had become bedridden and who had finally given up his courageous fight against the terrible disease of cancer.

As she and Oliver walked down the long, tree-lined pathway she offered up a silent prayer of thanksgiving for her health—what was a minor blood condition compared to Bernie's suffering?—and for her robust happy son.

Gavin opened the front passenger door as they approached, and Adele got in without meeting his gaze, but she was moved by his gentle squeeze as she passed him. He *did* understand, he *was* offering his sympathy in a silent, unpatronising way, and above all he had the knack of making Oliver a very happy little boy. She felt guilty that she couldn't show her gratitude, but she was conscious of being fortunate in having such friends.

The block of flats looked even more impressive by daylight and when they reached Gavin's doorway Oliver was delighted to help dry Honey's paws on an old towel.

'We must take our wellies off too,' Adele said. 'I should have brought slippers.'

'I'm sure Mother or Viv will have a spare pair near enough your size. I'm afraid we can't accommodate Oliver, but it's good for children to go barefoot.'

'He does at home mostly and it's all carpeted,' Adele answered quickly, but at the same time wondering who on earth Viv might be.

Oliver was a little shy at first, and Adele shocked into silence, all her previous fears and suspicions culminating in a disappointment so great that she could only stare rudely at the black-haired, blue-eyed woman who was sitting by the fire, her feet up on a stool, a pillow behind her head. Her face was pale, accentuating the high cheek-bones and straight Roman nose.

Mrs Lascelles led Adele to her side.

'This is my step-daughter, Vivien Lascelles, Adele.'

'We've met, haven't we?' the woman acknowledged. 'Well, sort of—you're one of Gavin's beauties.'

Adele tried to compose herself. 'Just one of the clinic's nurses. I'm sorry if you're not well,' she added politely.

'I'm really much better now, here to recuperate after having a breast removed.'

'Thanks to my clinic and the mammogram,' Gavin cut in shortly. 'Viv was an unwilling client, decidedly anti- anything remotely concerned with hospitals, doctors or anything medical.'

Vivien Lascelles' blue eyes flickered over Adele, then with slow deliberation her gaze transferred to Gavin.

'I'm only interested in people, darling,' she answered softly. Her look did not waver from her step-brother's face, and Adele wished she could have read the meaning behind their exchanged glances. It was Gavin who turned away first.

'Typical of a woman,' he muttered awkwardly, 'you're all so damned obstinate.'

It was the first time Adele had seen her boss at a disadvantage. He still had the last word, he always would, but this raven-haired beauty knew how to manage him. Hadn't Adele thought at first sight of Vivien that they were man and wife, if only by common law. Certainly they were on intimate terms, with an immediate rapport which shattered all Adele's dreams.

'That was all very quick,' Adele said, trying not to show her feelings. 'It seems like only yesterday that you were at the clinic for your screening.'

'We don't waste any time,' Gavin said, 'especially when the client happens to be as unwilling as Viv was.'

'But you were right, darling—and I am grateful,' Vivien crooned, holding out her hand to Gavin who took it and patted it gently.

'We can't have our own family letting us down now, can we?' He pulled away and turned his attention to Oliver who was clinging to Adele's side.

'No kite-flying today, young man, what would you like to do instead?'

Oliver swung one foot and tightened his hold on Adele's hand, shaking his head. 'Nothing,' he whispered, but as soon as Gavin stooped to make a fuss of Honey, Oliver quickly went up to him.

Mrs Lascelles went to Vivien's room to find a pair of slippers for Adele and Adele learned from Vivien that she had come out of hospital only a few days earlier.

'Lassie's taking me back with her tomorrow for a month's convalescence, then I have to see about work.'

'Lassie being our nickname for Mother,' Gavin intervened from somewhere across the room. 'She's far too young-looking to be recognised as 'Mother' and Lassie seems to fit.'

'I agree it does,' Adele said with a laugh as Mrs Lascelles returned with some warm fluffy mules.

'Everyone calls me Lassie,' she acknowledged with a smile. 'Makes me sound like a dog—maybe Honey and I should exchange names, anyway, Adele, you must use it too, I don't answer to Mrs Lascelles except on formal occasions. And you, my girl,' to Vivien, 'can forget about work for at least three months. The first thing is to find you a flat, though why you can't stay with me at Cedar Grove I can't imagine.'

'Because I like City life, as you well know, Lassie,' Vivien insisted. 'I have to be doing something.'

'Viv is a dress designer and she owns a model agency, Adele,' Lassie explained. 'Well, she has a partner who runs the London agency and Viv has just opened up here in the Midlands.'

'It's taken all of my profits, but I've been pressurised into taking things easier from now on, and Gavin has decided I have to be where he can keep an eye on me.'

'Where does Mrs Lascelles live exactly?' Adele asked, finding references to Gavin and Vivien's relationship a little off-putting. They were only step-brother and sister, neither of them married, but certainly possessive about each other, she observed.

'About thirty miles north of the City, beautiful countryside, very woody, and I have a large house in rural grounds, you must get Gavin to bring you out for a weekend, Adele,' Mrs Lascelles invited.

'A child's paradise, Adele,' Gavin agreed. 'Oliver would adore it.'

Mrs Lascelles went away then to prepare tea, leaving Vivien and Adele to become acquainted. Adele found Vivien an easy person to talk to even though she was, she discovered, ten years her senior.

A small but adequate dining room, furnished in pinewood furniture, led off from the kitchen where they assembled round a long table, sitting on chairs with rush seats and tall slim backs. Adele found it difficult to equate this apartment as being a bachelor one. It was homely and did not lack a woman's touch. She found herself wondering if in fact Vivien frequently shared it with Gavin, yet she had intimated that she needed to find somewhere else to live.

It cropped up again over tea when Gavin jovially suggested that he and Oliver were outnumbered by the fair sex.

'You can get Viv off my back, Adele,' he said, smiling generously from the end of the long table with Oliver next to him. 'You have a delightful flat going spare, and you must need some company.'

'I'd be a ready-made baby-sitter too,' Vivien offered eagerly, and Adele woke up to the realisation that this was yet another of Dr Gavin Forbes's decrees. It was all cut and dried, and she had been too naive to see how she was being used.

'But it's terribly small,' she protested quickly.

'You showed me over it and I thought it was adequate for one person, especially someone like Viv who is a business woman.'

'If Jacques, he's my partner, comes down he can always stay here with Gavin, and when I need a rest I can go to Lassie's.'

'It wasn't an addition to our house to sub-let,' Adele insisted.

'At least it would help with the rates,' Vivien said helpfully, and the pros and cons were discussed until Gavin drove Adele home, accompanied by Mrs Lascelles and Vivien who stayed for coffee after they had viewed the flat, and finally left at nine-thirty, having succeeded in persuading Adele to let Vivien live there at least until she could find somewhere else.

Adele was thankful that Matthew called the following evening and she wasted no time in airing her views.

'Dr Forbes has got a bloody cheek,' she exploded, ignoring Matthew's pained expression. 'He thinks he can ride rough-shod over me, use me, make me do anything he wants me to.'

'He's not exactly asking you to sell up and go to the Outer Hebrides, my dear,' Matthew replied quietly.

'Just because I work for him doesn't mean he owns me.'

Matthew raised his eyebrows, a faint smile reflected in his tender blue eyes which Adele refused to respond to.

'I know it was just coincidence when we met on the hill, but now Oliver's nuts about the wretched man and to come here and take charge—damn the man!' she fumed, 'on a pretext of his mother wanting to meet Oliver, taking us to his place for tea and only because his step-sister needs somewhere to live.' She paced the kitchen floor as Matthew stood framed in the doorway, patiently allowing her to let off steam. 'Step-sister indeed!' she continued. 'Why can't she live with *him*?—she's staying there at present, and his mother, so he must have adequate room.'

'Gavin is sleeping on the couch so that Vivien can have a room to herself to be quiet after the operation.'

Adele swung round to face Matthew.

'So you've met her?' she accused.

'I operated on her, Adele,' Matthew replied quietly. 'Vivien is a charming woman. Admittedly she was sceptical about *A Votre Santé* clinic in the beginning. It was Gavin who persuaded her to have a screening—the mammogram proved positive and you know the rest. I expect Gavin has told you that his step-father, Vivien's father, died from cancer. She has cause to be grateful to Gavin and his mother.'

'I'm sorry,' Adele replied shortly, 'but that isn't any concern of mine. Gavin Forbes is taking advantage of my position. Bernie and I had no intention of letting the flat.'

'Then you only had to politely refuse.'

Adele groaned angrily. 'It isn't as easy as that, Matthew. I did try—honestly, but—he—he just takes over.'

'You're a funny girl,' Matthew said. 'It's time you and Gavin had lost all your inhibitions, you know. Can't think why you've got such a chip where he's concerned.'

'I don't like having my life regulated for me,' she said sombrely.

Matthew grunted. 'No wonder I haven't found a woman then,' he said. 'I thought that was just what women did like—men who are masterful. I've evidently got it all wrong.'

Adele laughed at Matthew's unusual display of self-examination.

'I shouldn't worry about it,' she said flippantly, 'and don't try to change.'

He had walked a few paces back from the table, now he returned to her side with one long stride.

'Does that mean I'm in with a fifty-fifty chance, my dear? You know, Adele, I could love you a lot.'

'We'll have none of that,' Adele replied in mock rebuke, giving him a push.

'Bernie was a very lucky man,' Matthew said.

'No—*I* was the lucky one, which is why no other man will ever be able to take his place, Matthew. At least not for a very long time,' she added thoughtfully.

Matthew grunted again. 'I'm glad you're leaving room for change, my dear. Change creeps up unbidden, which is probably fortuitous for most of us.'

He grasped her arms, holding her still. 'Now you've got it all out of your system—you have, haven't you? How about a drink?'

He continued to hold her fast and bent to kiss her lightly

on her brow, then with his arm round her shoulder he walked her to the lounge where he poured a whisky for himself, and a sherry for Adele.

'You do need a woman's company, Adele—you need to get out more without Oliver.'

'Oh, don't start all that again,' she moaned dispassionately. 'I went to work and sent Oliver to nursery school to please you, and look at the trouble it's got me into.'

'Now you're being absurd, my dear. It is all doing you a lot of good and would be even better if you stopped fighting against it. To be happy in life you have to give of yourself. You're young and lovely, you have a lot to give.'

'I hope you're not suggesting that I start husband hunting,' she snapped impatiently.

'You wouldn't need to hunt, my dear. Just be yourself and the man will come to you,' he replied cryptically.

Throughout the week she felt restless, wanting life to go on just as if Bernie were alive, yet in more rational moments recognising that what Gavin had suggested was sensible and in her own interest. Inflation being what it was it was sensible to earn her keep by working, and in the cause of economics right to allow the rent of the flat help in the maintenance of Beecroft. She was well provided for, and Oliver too, but money was losing its value all the time. She knew that Matthew and Gavin were giving her good advice, so she cleaned the rooms of the flat, washed the curtains, polished the furniture. It was solid and well-preserved and helped the flat to have a cosy appearance.

Adele felt exhausted by the weekend, so when one of the mothers at nursery school suggested that Oliver went to her son's birthday party, which coincided with Hallowe'en on the Friday evening, Adele decided to take Oliver and leave him there even though she was invited too.

They shopped in the afternoon for a suitable present and Adele bought him a hideous mask and a witch's hat to take to the party, and at four o'clock she left him in the care of Jonathan's parents.

Over the past few weeks she had been pressurised into going for a session at the gym and afterwards relaxing in the sauna while Oliver stayed with one of the other girls at the clinic, Matthew, or even Gavin on two occasions.

She enjoyed going round the gym where the instructor supervised her on the various types of equipment, checked her weight, and helped devise a body-building programme, and she had to admit she felt better for these visits both mentally and physically. Gail Patterson, Jonathan's mother had laughingly suggested that Adele would enjoy a few hours to herself, so now she drove into town to the Health Club adjacent to the clinic.

There were hardly any other clients there. Adele presumed this was because it was nearing tea-time, but after she had been round the gym she seemed the only one to go into the sauna and this she decided must be because everyone was going to Hallowe'en parties.

The club was divided into separate departments for men and women, so after a refreshing shower she went into the sauna, spread out her towel and lay full length on her stomach. On occasion she had found it too hot to stay more than a few minutes between cold showers, but today it was just right and she rested comfortably.

After ten minutes she roused herself to go outside to have a shower and then she returned to the sauna, this time lying on her back.

All her cares and worries of the past week seemed to just float away and she felt completely at peace. She ran her finger idly down her moist flesh, remembering her first visit and how she'd covered herself with a huge bath sheet. But she quickly realised that everyone felt some embarrassment the first time and seeing the other members casually strolling about without even a towel Adele soon lost her shyness too. There was nothing in the world, she decided, quite so relaxing as lying stark naked in this embalming heat, allowing the pores of the skin to open and get rid of the hidden dirt.

Lying here, stretched out and becoming gradually dozy she became aware of herself as a woman. She felt an agony of desire as she realised how long it was since she had experienced a man's caresses.

Not so long though, she remembered, for Gavin Forbes had kissed her, and shown her why she was a woman.

The memories came hell-bent on making her conscious of her own weakness, of the need for a man's love . . .

CHAPTER SIX

MEMORIES roused and soothed alternately and only the click of the door brought Adele awake with the realisation that she had remained in the sauna too long. She struggled to get up, her mind fuzzy, her vision blurred, an intense nausea rising from the pit of her stomach. She rolled off the bench in drunken stupor and fought to reach the door—but black darkness engulfed her and she crumpled into a heap on the floor.

She was aware of murmuring voices as she came to, and someone was pushing her head down to her knees. For a second or two she couldn't remember where she was and then as she began to focus she recognised the tiled floor, the non-slip covering outside the row of shower cubicles.

Then a man's brisk tread outside, a draught of cold air and a commanding voice.

'What's going on? Adele? Are you all right?'

'She fainted, sir. We didn't realise she was still in there. One of the instructresses decided to come for a shower and found Adele staggering about in the sauna.'

'You silly girl,' Gavin admonished curtly. 'What possessed you to stay so long—you know fifteen minutes is long enough.'

'I . . . I think I must have fallen asleep,' Adele managed to say.

'Just as well I was still in my office.'

'She didn't seem to come round quickly like most people do,' the instructress said, 'so we thought it best to see if a doctor was still at the clinic.'

'I'm glad you did. Come along, Adele, let's get you into a warm place.'

He swept her up in his arms as she clutched at the bath sheet which thankfully someone had placed round her. Now she was shivering, and as he set her down on one of the elongated relaxing chairs in the nearby lounge Adele frantically drew the towel closer.

The girls hadn't followed, she was alone with Gavin Forbes. She couldn't face him; instead she whispered: 'I'm sorry.'

'Nothing to be sorry about, fair damsel, but you must take more care.'

His hands were sliding over the bath sheet as he massaged her arms and legs, gently stimulating the blood flow.

'You might feel less queasy over the other way,' he suggested softly, but as she turned over the bath sheet fell apart and he spread it over the chair, his fingers gently manipulating her neck, her shoulders, her arms, and she found it intolerably soothing. He massaged her back briskly at first, then with more tender suppleness, his fingers hovering at her side beneath her arms.

'Feel better now?' he whispered in her ear.

She could feel his warm breath on her neck as he leaned over her and his nearness made her go weak again.

'Yes, I'm fine now,' she said huskily.

'What were you doing here at this time?'

'Oliver's at a party. A birthday party incorporating Hallowe'en. I was supposed to go back at about seven to join them.'

'Are you quite dry?' He ran slender fingers meaningfully down the length of her until she shuddered.

'Cold?' he asked quickly.

'No,' she said shaking her head, gathering up a handful of bath sheet, but before she could turn over he enclosed her in his arms leaving the bath sheet spread out on the chair as he stood her down in front of him.

She hugged her arms about her, and dared to look into his eyes, eyes that had turned a deep shade of greeny-blue, sparkling with pleasure.

'You're glowing nicely,' he muttered into her tousled and damp hair, 'but you shuddered, fair damsel, and I like that. I like it very much.'

'Only because—' Adele began.

'Because I found a sensitive spot? You're human after

all, and that I find most encouraging.'

He took her hands in his, forcing them apart to expose the front of her, and she was grateful for the diffused lighting which hid her scarlet cheeks as he looked and smiled in approval.

'It's all there,' he teased, running two fingers from thigh to breast and cupping it with his hand.

Adele started to protest and pull away, but he hugged her passionately. 'The fairest damsel in all the world,' he crooned and then patting her bottom added: 'I think we'd better get you home.'

Adele made a grab for the bath sheet. 'I'm perfectly all right, really, Gavin—there was no need—' and her voice died away as he placed his hands on her bare shoulders and gazed affectionately into her eyes.

'I don't have my car here,' he said. 'I'll run you home, then pick Oliver up.'

'I'll go and dress and then see how I feel,' she insisted.

'I'll be waiting in reception.'

He went out, his step less decisive than usual, and she pulled the huge bath sheet tightly round her, and into a ball in which she buried her face.

What was happening to her? Of all people why had the girls sent for Gavin Forbes? She had only fainted from prolonged heat, but she had felt quite ill for a few moments. She hurried to the changing room and unlocked her locker, remembering her deodorant, talc and a spot or two of perfume. The sauna made her skin feel smooth and clean, and now she wanted to make the best of herself.

Everyone was concerned about her, but assured her that it was quite a common occurrence until you got thoroughly used to regular saunas, and she thanked the girls for their trouble, and went out to reception where Gavin was talking to the manager of the men's side of the club. She braced herself, imagining that a variety of cryptic remarks might be launched towards her, but Gavin greeted her as if they had met by design for the first time that evening.

'I hope you haven't hurried on my account, darling,' he said, and Adele noticed the manager raise an eyebrow suspiciously. Gavin took her arm as he led her down the spiral staircase to the subway below. The evenings were dark now, but it was a cold, clear, star-studded night.

'I'm sure I'm being an awful nuisance, Gavin,' Adele suggested humbly. 'I'm really quite capable of driving myself home. In any case there's this party.'

'What time were they expecting you?' he asked.

'I said about seven—it's past that now and the children's session was to end around seven. Gail wanted me to get a baby-sitter so that I could go back, or let Oliver sleep with Jonathan, but I wasn't keen. I wouldn't know anyone there.'

'Don't let me stop you, Adele—perhaps I could gate-crash.'

'I'm sure you could,' she agreed with a laugh. 'It sounded like that kind of party, but I'd rather get Oliver home to bed. He'll be tired and excited.'

'It's Saturday tomorrow,' he said nonchalantly.

'I know, but—well—I really don't want to go to the party,' she said making a face.

She didn't enlighten Gavin that up until her ill-fated sauna she'd had every intention of going to the party, but now Gavin's company seemed a more inviting way to spend the evening.

They picked Oliver up en route and he fell asleep almost at once, so Gavin carried him in to the house and he was soon tucked up in his own bed.

Adele made coffee and found a few snacks to eat.

'Have you missed a meal?' she asked Gavin when he wandered into the kitchen to see what she was doing.

When he didn't answer she glanced up at him and found him grinning fiendishly.

'The hors d'oeuvre I had has given me an appetite for the rest of the meal,' he replied saucily.

She turned away quickly, wondering if after all she was capable of handling such a man as Gavin Forbes.

He crept up behind her and despite her squeals tantalised her with kisses, his face buried in her neck, his hands clasped round her tiny waist.

Midst her protests and laughter she rebuked his frivolity. 'You'll wake Oliver,' she said.

'Never,' he answered brashly, 'but to be serious, fair damsel, I did have an excellent business lunch, so coffee and a snack will be splendid.'

'Won't your mother and Vivien be expecting you home?'

'Lassie and Viv are back at Cedar Grove—I'm a lonely bachelor again. Viv will stay with Mother for about four weeks before she comes to you. If that's convenient, of course?'

'Yes, any time. I've spring-cleaned—I suppose that should be autumn-cleaned—the flat.'

'Working too hard?—that the reason you fell asleep in the sauna?'

Adele shrugged. 'Could be,' but she remembered the provocative thoughts she'd had which had lulled her into unconsciousness.

Gavin carried the tray into the lounge and Adele followed with the coffee pot. He closed the double glass doors softly, and then leaning across the settee pulled Adele round to the open space in the centre of the room. She looked at him questioningly, and in reply his lips met hers, deliciously soft and enticing at first, and then his mouth urged hers to a unison of inflamed sensuality. He demanded, Adele gave; all the passion and love which she had stored away flooded her being and responded to Gavin's tempting. 'I want you, fair damsel—God, how I want you.'

He caught her lips between his own several times in quick succession, the expression in his eyes tender as he courted her weakening will-power.

Without being aware of her actions she had slid her hands underneath his jacket and the feel of his warm muscular body afforded the comfort so long denied her.

Still holding her with one firm hand he loosened his tie, took it off and tossed it on to the settee, then he shrugged off his jacket and placed it over the back of the settee. Ardent kisses followed, the kind that made her feel as if he was drawing every ounce of passion from deep inside her. Then he unzipped the tunic of her trouser-suit and the dainty bra presented no barrier as he discarded both items, draping them too over the back of the settee.

'Oliver might come down,' she croaked in fear of her own actions as well as those of Gavin Forbes.

'Does he ever?'

'Well—no—'

'But you're anticipating a first time?'

'I wouldn't like him to—'

'He's fast asleep and you know it—we could be too—in say—half an hour's time?' he suggested wickedly.

He forced her head back, kissing her throat, along her shoulder blades until she was senseless again, except that she could feel her breasts swelling in response to his thrilling touch, and the rest of her body was throbbing with expectation.

'Shall we go upstairs for dessert?' he asked with a smile.

Adele rested her head against his chest, hugging him, caressing his broad back and savouring every inch of him yet knowing that she must stop before it was too late.

She wanted him, she craved to unleash his virility, to be caught up together and held on the high wire of suspense, but she was afraid. With Bernie love had come first. This man was out to show his prowess as a virile, non-compromising lover. He wanted her just as he would want any other woman whose defences were down, and whom he could exploit. Love didn't seem to come into it. Perhaps he loved Vivien and he had used his persuasive charm to get his step-sister the flat so that they would be near each other. He too, it seemed, guarded his reputation jealously, yet both he and Matthew were scheming to use Beecroft for their own indulgences.

'The coffee's getting cold,' Adele said drawing herself away and hating the emptiness of her arms. She picked up the tunic top and put it on zipping it up to the neck, but Gavin simply came behind her and unzipped it again.

'Oh no you don't, fair damsel,' he said close to her ear. 'You have the right to deny me dessert, but not the table decoration.'

He searched for and found the weakening nerve just

below her ear, and she quivered involuntarily.

'You want me as much as I want you, my darling,' he said softly. 'But don't think that I am going to put up with you stringing me along in the way that you've taunted Matthew.'

It took her a few moments to comprehend this, then she lashed out with tongue and fists indignantly.

'You've got it all wrong,' she accused. 'There's never been anything between Matthew and me—I've told you that before. How dare you take advantage—'

He held her fiercely against him then he shook her as bitter defeat angered him.

'Don't *you* dare accuse me of taking advantage, my girl, any more than you can Matthew. What the bloody hell do you think men are made of, for God's sake? Matthew may have the patience of a saint but I'm not made that way. I want you, Adele—'

'No you don't,' she screamed at him, incensed with humiliation as he forced her back over the settee, his eyes devouring every inch of white flesh. 'Any woman could serve your purpose—any slut off the street.'

She cried out in anguish as his hand whipped across her cheek.

'Don't you dare speak to me like that,' he roared. 'Your pent-up emotions are causing you to be irrational.'

His face was burning with wrath as he ran his fingers through his hair.

Adele dissolved into weeping; she crept away into a corner of the room and sobbed violently. Never in her life had she been in such a situation. Gavin had struck her. Apart from the physical hurt, he had caused her mental pain. The desire she had experienced for him meant only that she loved him and now she knew for sure because she was distraught at her rejection of him. The confusion in her heart was making her behave out of character. She longed for this hateful man so desperately, and yet she was afraid to love him, afraid of the mutual passion which had been in danger of a sexual union which she might later discover was merely lust on his part.

She shrugged her tunic top back on and zipped it up. 'Please go,' she pleaded.

'Come and have your coffee,' he said icily, his voice still full of the contempt he felt for her. 'It's poured out.'

She went slowly to the low table and picked up her cup and saucer.

Gavin was actually eating a sausage roll. Men could be infuriating, with feelings only skin deep, she thought.

'Sit down,' he commanded brutally. 'I am not the sort of man to tolerate stupidity, Adele. There are times when I think you simply haven't grown up.' He glanced up at her as she stood hovering after taking one sip of nearly cold coffee and replacing the cup and saucer on the tray. He grabbed her and pulled her down beside him. 'You're a woman, for heaven's sake—and a damned desirable one, but the way you carry on is asking for rape. You realise that—don't you?'

'No,' she answered pointedly. 'The men in my life have been men of impeccable good manners.'

'Then they're not normal—sooner or later Matthew would have—my God, Adele—what do you suppose he comes here for?'

'Certainly not the same as you. Not all men are potential rapists,' she flung at him. 'Matthew has been like a father to me.'

'Hgh!' Gavin scoffed. 'You'd better come down to earth fast.'

'Just because I happen to be a young widow with a nice home, and the means to live decently doesn't mean I intend to hold open house for the likes of—every bachelor in the neighbourhood.'

She had been going to say 'for the likes of you' but his scowling face warned her of another intended assault.

He placed his empty cup and saucer on the tray with a clatter, stood up and with a curt: 'Good night, Adele,' stalked out of the room.

Adele heard the front door close. She was stunned, unable to believe what was happening. A few minutes later she dashed to the front door, opened it and seeing her car in the drive ran to the gate, but away down the road she could just see the shadow of a man's figure walking briskly along in the moonlight. She couldn't chase after him, not even in the car, there was Oliver to consider, in bed asleep.

Her feet dragged on the driveway as she locked up the car and left it where it was before going inside and securing the front door.

She shivered with the cold and went back to the lounge where she drank her coffee in one gulp. She tried to remember whether he had been wearing a car coat—no, just his suit—he would be cold, but common-sense told her that he could easily get a taxi if he wanted to.

She felt wretched. Of course he wasn't the kind of man to want sex of any woman he happened to meet, but he hadn't mentioned love either. A man's needs were different, sex was important to them and all she wanted was love and security. She felt guilty because she had readily responded to Gavin's advances. She tried to analyse her feelings. She had believed she would never love again. She wasn't ready for such emotion yet her body had proved otherwise. Gavin was domineering and arrogant—yet her heart was inextricably drawn to him. In every way he was vastly different from Bernie. Comparing them Bernie seemed so immature yet he had proved himself to be an astute businessman and clever craftsman. They had been young lovers, now, inevitably she supposed a second love would have of necessity to be a love of a different kind. Could she cope? Would she ever be able to come to terms with the changes life had forced upon her? It didn't matter, because Gavin had gone out of her life and she couldn't blame him. Her accusations were inexcusable. There was still Matthew, of course, gentle and caring, but Gavin had suggested that eventually he would make demands. What then?

The walk home would calm Gavin down, she consoled, then he would ring and apologise. She ought to apologise too, but who would make the first move? How was she going to face him at the clinic? Thank goodness there was the weekend first, but how was she going to get through that knowing that she had upset the man who was beginning to mean something special to her.

The telephone did not ring and Adele slept fitfully, impatient with Oliver early next morning when he crept into her bed for a cuddle just when she had gone off to sleep.

Eventually when the teasmade proclaimed its duty done she roused to switch off the alarm. She caught sight of herself in the mirror. Scrawny neck, she observed, her slimness now hidden beneath a brushed nylon nightdress and woollen bed-jacket—not much to allure a man with, she thought sulkily. Sleeping alone after years of having a human furnace next to you was something she would never enjoy. She gave a deep, discontented sigh before pouring out tea for herself and Oliver.

'What's the matter, Mummy?' Oliver asked in concern.

'A bit of a headache—I stayed in the sauna too long yesterday.'

Oliver was always the same. Once he was awake he was lively and eager to chatter. She listened as he told her all about Jonathan's party, and she thought back over the past couple of months and was amazed at the change in him. He seemed to have blossomed into a very independent little boy. He was frequently mischievous, even naughty at times which Matthew assured her was right, and quite normal. Every morning at breakfast time he reminded Adele to take her red pill. She knew that over the last couple of days she had been feeling better, but now after the incident with Gavin she felt miserable. She had to control her feelings. It was so easy to take out her unhappiness on Oliver, and in turn that made him rebel so although she would have preferred a day at home spent quietly without having to meet anyone, when Oliver suggested they ought to be getting ready to go to The Golden Eagle, she agreed for his sake.

As they didn't stop to do any shopping they reached the restaurant where they often had Saturday lunch, in the middle of the busiest period so had to wait about ten minutes for their table.

Donald Paradine, the manager, suggested they wait in

the comfortable reception lounge and personally fetched an orange juice for Oliver and a sherry for Adele.

'You're looking well if I may say so, Mrs Kinsey,' he said pleasantly.

Adele managed what she considered must be a sickly smile, wondering if looks could be that deceptive or was Donald just being kind?

He chatted to Oliver before he was called away and by the time they had half-finished their drinks returned to tell them that their table was ready. He brought a small tray and carried their half-filled glasses to the table ahead of them.

Adele acknowledged one or two people whom she knew, but the restaurant was crowded and service unusually slow. She felt slightly revived after finishing her sherry but Oliver began to get fidgetty.

'I'm hungry,' he announced in a loud voice.

'We came a little too early so we'll have to be patient.' She was looking through the menu, trying to find something tempting. 'Shall we have roast pork and apple sauce for a change today?'

Oliver struggled to push back his chair which refused to budge on the thick carpet so that he pulled the tablecloth askew as he got down, shouting: 'There's him—Mummy, there's him!'

Adele felt her inside go cold and her rebuke to Oliver went unheeded as he squeezed between potted palms and exotic ferns to get to the plate glass window.

She followed Oliver's gaze and sure enough there was the back of Gavin Forbes. He was talking to a family of people Adele recognised as having left the restaurant a short time ago. Oliver began to call: 'I'm here—*I'm here*,' as he tapped the window urgently.

Adele began to get up as people were looking, some slightly amused at Oliver's self-importance and then she sat down hurriedly again as Gavin turned and looked into the window.

'Hullo—I'm just going to have my dinner—can you come too?' Oliver called excitedly.

'Darling, please,' Adele begged, 'come and sit down, here's your soup coming,' but Oliver turned and rushed between the tables, getting in the way of the waiters and causing a furore, and when Adele glanced again out of the windows which spanned the length of the restaurant she saw Gavin mounting the stone steps outside two at a time. She felt herself go limp, but the waiter placed a bowl of soup in front of her.

'Should I go after him, Mrs Kinsey?' he asked.

Adele stretched her neck to look over other people's heads towards the door.

'No, I think he's okay—it's someone he knows,' she explained as she saw the tall figure of Gavin coming into the restaurant holding Oliver's hand.

She had no time to reason with herself or plan how she would react, Gavin was there, helping Oliver back into his seat and then looking down at her.

'May I?' he asked, indicating one or other of the two vacant chairs.

She wanted to quip that it was a free country but that would have been churlish, and Oliver intervened.

'You sit there,' he ordered, 'in my Daddy's place.'

Gavin smiled so affectionately at Oliver that Adele's heart melted.

'Do you think he would mind?' Gavin asked Oliver.

'No, no—'cos he's not coming back,' Oliver assured Gavin.

'And how is Mummy today?' Gavin asked searching her face directly.

'She's not very well,' Oliver announced. 'She's got a headache.'

'Mummy will have to remember not to fall asleep in the sauna,' Gavin advised, still not taking his gaze from Adele, who briefly responded to his jibe. She noticed in that momentary glance that Gavin looked tired. He normally looked youthful and the picture of health, but today there was a heaviness around his eyes.

'Can I get you something, sir?' the waiter asked, returning to their table.

'Have you ordered, Adele?' Gavin enquired.

'Only the soup,' she explained.

'Mummy said we could have roast pork and apple sauce,' Oliver chipped in.

'Then soup, please,' Gavin ordered, 'roast pork and apple sauce for three, followed by three knickerbocker glory's—but with a slight rest between dinner and dessert.'

Adele felt her heartbeats flutter at the word 'dessert' and she couldn't bring herself to look at Gavin, but despite her glowing cheeks continued drinking her soup, keeping one eye on Oliver at the same time.

All the more pleasant side of the previous evening came back to mind and she sensed that Gavin had deliberately reminded her of those few passion-filled moments.

Oliver began chattering again and Adele reprimanded him for talking instead of eating.

'You get on with *your* soup,' Oliver returned to her precociously. '*I* want to talk to "him".'

Gavin was forced to look away, his eyes brimmed full of laughter as Adele scolded: 'Oliver! Dr Forbes has a name—it's very rude to refer to "him".'

The waiter arrived with Gavin's soup and as Gavin began to enjoy the steaming contents of the bowl he leaned towards Oliver.

'Let's just make it Gavin, shall we? We're buddies after all.'

'Oh no!' Adele protested in horror. 'That would be dreadfully disrespectful, and he might do it to someone else.'

Oliver looked from one to the other.

'Then perhaps I could be a special sort of Uncle?' Gavin suggested.

Oliver remained thoughtful. 'Well, I haven't got a Daddy,' he said with feeling.

Gavin reached across and lifted the little boy's chin, smiling at the stained mouth and brown moustache comprising of soup interlaced with dashes of orange squash.

'Daddys, Oliver, are *very* special people,' Gavin explained. 'I think we'll let that ride for a bit as I'm sure your

Mummy would like to choose one for you, when she's ready and feeling better.'

'She wouldn't mind,' Oliver insisted, shaking his head solemnly, 'really—and it would save her the bother of choosing,' he added convincingly.

'Dr Forbes won't come out to dinner with you again because you're talking too much, Oliver,' Adele rebuked firmly.

Oliver looked suitably rebuffed and gazed sadly into his soup bowl while Gavin ruffled his hair.

When the next course was served Oliver ate quickly enjoying his meal in anticipation of what was to come.

There was a silence between Gavin and Adele, but not an awkward one, and after Gavin had called the wine waiter and ordered a bottle of wine, and more orange squash for Oliver he said:

'Mother would like you to go out to Cedar Grove for a long weekend—you and Oliver, of course.'

'It's very kind of her—' Adele began, frantically trying to think up an excuse to refuse the invitation.

'Before you say anything, I had better confirm that you haven't changed your mind about the flat?'

'I don't usually go back on my word,' Adele said frostily.

'Good—then we thought towards the end of November. I'll drive you out there on the Friday afternoon and we'll return on Sunday—I'm sorry I can't allow you time off—I have to get back myself anyway—bringing Viv back with us.'

Adele ate anticipating the difficulties such a weekend would present. After last evening they could never be the same again. He was only being reasonable now because he was fond of Oliver and because he needed the flat at Beecroft for Vivien. She supposed once Vivien was installed at Beecroft Gavin would call only to visit his step-sister and even Oliver would have to take a back seat. Thank goodness there was a separate entrance with stairs between the house and garage. The flat's lounge was an integral part of the house with a door opening on to the landing, but that, Adele felt sure, Vivien would keep locked from the inside.

Gradually she had been coming round to the idea of having someone at hand. It was an ideal solution, especially as Vivien was a new acquaintance, so that Adele did not have to feel under any obligation to her.

Oliver tugged at Adele's sleeve and she leaned across for him to whisper in her ear.

'Too much orange squash,' Adele laughed in response. 'Excuse yourself, darling, and don't forget to wash your hands. Take a tissue and wash your mouth while you're there.'

When Oliver had skipped off through the now less crowded restaurant, Gavin asked: 'Would you like me to go with him or will he be all right?'

Adele was watching her son with concern, then she turned to Gavin and smiled, forgetting any previous animosity between them. 'No, Donald Paradine has taken him—they're so nice here.'

She had finished eating and as she placed her fork by the side of her knife she sighed. 'We'll have to change that order and make it only two knickerbocker glory's. In fact I'm not at all sure that Oliver—'

'Be quiet,' Gavin rebuked sharply. 'Of course he can, and so will you.' He placed his hand over hers on the table and looked intently into her eyes. 'I hoped I'd find you here today. I came to apologise, Adele, my behaviour last evening was unforgivable—all the same I am begging you to do just that. This may be hard for you to understand, but I have never *ever* struck a woman before, and I hope, please God, I shall never be provoked into doing so again.'

'It's I who should apologise—' she began, feeling a lump rising in her throat.

'The situation was charged with emotion,' he said cutting her short. 'I can only assume it blew up as a result of intense frustration. We are both in a vulnerable position.'

She looked at him hopefully, but again he refused to allow her to speak.

'We have to work together, and I feel now that I have a certain obligation to Oliver, of whom you must be proud and I am certainly very fond. If he has inherited his father's charm then I can well understand why you are loathe to extinguish the candle you hold so dearly to Bernie's memory. I do not wish ever to be reminded of last evening, Adele, the matter is closed.'

CHAPTER SEVEN

ADELE did not wish the matter to be closed, but before she could speak Oliver came running back to the table with a waiter close behind, and a few moments later they were all three delving into the cold delights of a knickerbocker glory.

When Adele had almost emptied her glass she noticed that Gavin had already finished.

'There you are, fair damsel,' he said charmingly. 'It wasn't that difficult was it? In fact I'd say you enjoyed it as much as I did—and Oliver too.'

'It was refreshing—now we shall have to walk that off,' she said decisively.

'Will you come to the swing-park with us, Uncle Gavin?'

'Yes, of course, Oliver, but I won't be able to stay long as I have to visit my mother.'

'Do you visit her every weekend?' Adele asked.

Gavin paused and again seemed to be trying to read something from Adele's expression. 'When I have nothing better to do,' he said with a slight smirk.

Adele knew instantly by that smirk that he was referring to her accusation of him being eager for any slut off the streets. He had said the matter was closed, but he only intended to forget what he wanted to forget for his own pride, and that was that he had smacked a woman's face. Adele wanted to forget too, forget that she had made those accusations against him. She knew that she had been grossly unjust, for above all Gavin Forbes was an honourable man. He did have two sides though, the almost stern, professional manner, the businessman of high integrity, but away from the clinic he showed a leaning towards simple domesticity. He was good with Oliver—would be with all children, she thought, and wondered why he had not made paediatrics his speciality. There were quite a few 'why's' where Gavin was concerned. Such a home-loving man would surely consider marriage high on his list of priorities—and that brought Adele back to wondering about Gavin and his step-sister, Vivien. She let out an involuntary sigh—she would soon know what that relationship incurred once Vivien came to live at Beecroft.

'What's troubling you, Adele? That was a pretty potent sigh,' Gavin asked.

'Oliver's being slow,' she said, doing some quick thinking. 'Is it a bit much, Oliver?' she asked.

He beamed and shook his head, plunging the long spoon to the bottom of the glass and again Adele's heart was full of love for her offspring. In a curious way he was responsible for much of the domesticity between herself and Gavin.

It was flying the kite that had brought them together on a homely level in the first instance and now, today, if there hadn't been Oliver how would Gavin have apologised? It was pure speculation of course, but she doubted that he would have bothered.

Adele had similar thoughts too when they walked together to the swing-park. Passers-by glanced at them, assuming that they were an ordinary family and for a panic-stricken moment she wanted to yell: 'He's not my husband—my Bernie is dead.'

Bernie's death and the memories of him didn't taunt her so frequently of late, but when they did it was like a huge foaming, curling wave that washed over her and deluged her in a flood of loneliness.

How was it that Gavin knew of those moments?—and now in his usual protective way was gently squeezing her hand.

Oliver was already running on ahead through the small gate in the iron railings.

'It comes over you like the waves on the sea-shore, my darling,' Gavin whispered. 'And each time you imagine it has swallowed up a little more of you, but one day the tide changes, the waves decrease, and when the tide goes out again a little more is left of you, a little more strength develops, a bit more solidarity to last you over until the next tidal wave comes.'

Adele couldn't answer for the paralysing constriction of her voice, and she had to blink back the persistent moistness which filled her eyes, and which seemed to turn to ice as the keen east wind blew across the park.

Gavin let go her hand and ran after Oliver who in a few moments was swinging high in the air and by the time he had enjoyed several goes on the swings and slides Adele had composed herself.

Finally she stood by as Gavin swung Oliver up in his arms, saying: 'Now you be a good lad for your Mummy— I'll see you soon, Oliver. We'll have fun when you come to see Honey won't we?'

'When can I?' Oliver asked.

'When you get home, ask Mummy to show you the date on the calendar, Oliver, then you can tick off the days—it's quite a long time, but I daresay I shall see you before then.' He turned to Adele. 'You'll be seeing Matthew, I expect?'

'I expect,' Adele answered solemnly, knowing in her heart that it was Gavin she would rather be seeing.

She was surprised when he kissed her cheek lightly. So pleasantly surprised that her gaze met his undauntingly, responding to the genuine warmth of affection she saw in his eyes. Their lips came together automatically, his with a light brush at first, smooth, tantalising on her mouth, then as quickly drawn away, but compulsively returning as she effortlessly held her lips apart to drink from the luscious sensuousness of his, and then, without another word long determined strides took him away leaving Adele feeling somewhat forlorn.

The remainder of the weekend passed slowly, and the hopeless emptiness stayed with Adele, although she endeavoured to be bright for Oliver's sake.

Monday morning was wet with a fierce gale blowing as well, so Adele drove to Jonathan's home first to pick him up and then dropped the children off at nursery school. On fine days she left Oliver with Jonathan, and his mother walked the two little boys, who were now firm friends, to the school.

She reached the clinic in good time making the most of

the opportunity to tidy herself after the walk from the car park. The clinic did sport a car park at the rear of the buildings, but being in the centre of the city it was only large enough to hold half a dozen cars, and these spaces were reserved for the doctors.

As she viewed her cheeks in the mirror, glowing from the sting of rain beating into her face, she remembered the impact of Gavin's hand across her cheek. She wondered what her colleagues would make of it, but for all she knew they might have gone through a similar experience with their boss. Adele threw out such an idea as preposterous. There was Vivien. It altered all her fantasies about Gavin Forbes. He was already spoken for, and by his step-sister who obviously dominated him. That same step-sister was destined to share Beecroft with Adele and Oliver.

She peered closer into the mirror, brushing her eyelids with green eye-shadow, well aware that she was green with envy of Vivien Lascelles. She didn't feel any animosity towards her. Viv was too likeable a person for that. A clear-headed, sophisticated business woman, but with a sparkling, friendly personality, even at present when she was not feeling her best. Adele experienced a dart of cold fear run through her heart as she put herself in Viv's shoes. Even now after the operation she must be afraid of what the future held. Didn't Adele know the futility of vain hope? The circumstances were different, of course, and how she congratulated Viv on her eager spirit to get back into the throes of business again with no time for those niggling doubts which must inevitably rise to the surface from time to time. She deserved Gavin, someone who would care for her, and love her . . . but such thoughts opened up a stab wound in Adele's heart. If he hadn't felt some affection for *her* would he have kissed her so fondly, so meaningfully, almost taking it for granted that he could persuade her to share a much more intimate relationship? Was he playing fast and loose with Vivien? Did he think that because Adele had been happily married she was now so sex-starved she would jump into bed with the first man who offered his services? The suggestions he had made about Matthew—

dear Matthew on whom she depended—did he really expect to be rewarded at the end of it all with what Gavin had suggested? Suddenly she hated all men, cursing them silently for being mercenary enough to want her for her money, the material things she had, as well as for the satisfaction she might be able to provide.

It was still well before nine when Sheila hurried into the cloak-room, intruding into Adele's reflections.

'What a morning!' she greeted with a certain venom in her voice. 'The car wouldn't start, the leads must have been damp or something, but my husband has a thing about it being the battery—it's always the blasted battery so he just gives up. "Get the bus," he says in his own placid way, so after a flaming row I did.'

'I thought you said he was placid,' Adele said with a laugh.

'That's the trouble, I have to pick a fight to make him unruffled—it's maddening.'

'You could have phoned me, Sheila—it wouldn't have been out of my way.'

Sheila pulled off her headscarf and looked at Adele.

'Adele, you look as if you've been here at least quarter of an hour. I did try Denise, but she must have already left so if I'd stopped to look up anyone else's number I'd have missed the bus. Just this morning when I wanted to be early.'

'What's so special about this morning?' Adele asked curiously.

'Doctor's conference—Dr Forbes has his office set out like a board room. Oh—he's so blasted efficient, he takes some keeping up with, and I can't go in there looking like this. They'll all be here on the stroke of nine. Oh—' she sighed, gazing into the mirror, 'it was such a super weekend too, and Colin isn't on duty at the hospital until this afternoon we could have gone on and on—'

Adele laughed. 'Now that sounds like over-indulgence.'

'Sorry love—it must be awful for you—I can't imagine life without Col. I must ring him and apologise for being such a pig. He ought to slap my face, I wish he would, but he

just isn't the sort—and he's on duty non-stop for the rest of
the week. The pressures of being a surgical registrar.'

Adele picked up her bag hiding the burning memory of
her own slapped face.

'I'll make a start on the post, shall I?' she asked, anxious
to change the subject.

'No—be a pet and give me a hand in Dr Forbes's room.
You go on in, put the chairs round his long table—the one
on the far side. I expect he'll have cleared it—he'll soon tell
you what to do. At least let him see that someone is ready
for work.'

Adele was glad that she had been early, grateful for those
extra few minutes to make the best of herself, and now
eager to see Gavin again.

She knocked and entered his office briskly. He was
standing by the official-looking oak table and half turned so
that his body muscles rippled beneath the elegant dark suit.

'Come and take the end of this,' he commanded brusque-
ly.

'Good morning,' Adele said.

'Lucky you if you can find anything good about it. Isn't
anyone conscientious enough to get here on time?' he
barked.

Adele took the end of the table and with impatience he
indicated that he wanted it moved over to the wide open
space by the window.

As they put it down, Adele, flushed and breathless said
'Sheila had to bus in, her car wouldn't start.'

'No excuse,' Gavin replied shortly. 'Everyone has to
make allowances for their personal commitments, and I
suspect the car was the least of Sheila's if Colin is off duty.
That's the trouble with employing married women, when it
isn't the family it's a demanding husband.' He paused and
looking down the length of the long table watched the
colour fade from Adele's face before it rushed back into her
cheeks. He gazed at her, intensely at first, his hard green
eyes gradually softening as if recognition was at last dawn-
ing, and his expression became full of compassion. What
was he remembering, she wondered? By the way his eyes

raked over her he was stripping her of her clothes, recalling her nakedness in the sauna. By the sudden relaxing of his lips he must be experiencing an encore of desire. She could almost feel the grip of his arms about her, the trembling anticipation of passion, but he was gripping the table fiercely as if to ward off the temptation.

He pulled himself up as if the strain were painful, then slowly and with his usual professional dignity he walked towards her.

'I'm sorry, my dear,' he said huskily. 'That was uncalled' for, unkind,' then with a crooked smile, he inclined his head. 'Of course, you did have an opportunity—'

He didn't mix business with pleasure she reminded herself, otherwise she would have fallen into his arms. They remained only inches apart, so close in spirit Adele felt sure, yet the atmosphere keeping them obliquely divorced.

Sheila burst in on them, effusing her apologies apparently unaware of the tension she had broken.

To have said the car wouldn't start ought to have been sufficient, but Sheila related the story word for word, and Gavin listened patiently turning away from Adele to look reluctantly at Sheila.

It wasn't the words which Sheila used, it was the implication which drew a knowing look from Gavin. In their exchanged glances Adele felt herself becoming consumed with yet more jealousy. Had those two been intimate too?

Sheila moved provocatively close to her boss, fussing with her scarf, and it seemed to Adele that Gavin watched every movement with paramount interest.

'I'm sorry you had to leave your paradise,' Gavin said when he could get a word in, a suggestive smile deepening the dimples in his cheeks. 'If you can cool your ardour perhaps we could all concentrate on the day's work.' To anyone else that would have been a sarcastic rebuke, but he sounded good-natured towards Sheila, leaving Adele feeling spurned. If only Sheila hadn't come in at that precise moment when the atmosphere had been charged with explosive—but what did she think might have happened? Gavin Forbes was not a man to forget himself. The clinic was his top priority, and ethics of the utmost importance.

'You can carry on with the post, Adele,' Sheila suggested.

'I think you can use a little help,' Gavin cut in officiously to Sheila. 'A good idea if Adele knows the routine for a meeting or conference—after all, one of these days you're going to—um—oversleep?'

Sheila's eyes were brimming with immodest implication, but Gavin turned and left the room abruptly.

'Clean paper and folders in the top drawer of the cabinet,' Sheila ordered. 'My God, I thought I'd be in for a rocket, but,' she added with a grin, 'any reference to sex wins *him* round. Lucky it was me that was late and not you, Adele. He thinks he's being terribly thoughtful in employing married nurses, and let's face it he pays us far more than the NHS would, but you're the first person we've had with a family. Definitely against the rules, so I'm warning you, he's likely to pounce for the least little thing.'

All the pleasure which Adele had gained from the brief encounter with Gavin vanished instantly. Whatever had or had not taken place between Gavin and Sheila, they did know one another very well. Did Sheila see Adele as a threat to her position? Was she annoyed that Gavin had suggested she learn the routine more thoroughly? Gavin had been slightly facetious in his remarks to Sheila, but Adele felt certain that really his chief concern was only that everything was prepared in good time for the conference.

When Adele walked back through reception the doctors had all arrived and were standing around in earnest conversation. She caught Matthew's eye and smiled, and instantly he broke away from his colleagues and with his arm around Adele's waist walked a few yards with her.

'You're looking particularly lovely this morning, my dear,' he said fondly.

Adele tut-tutted. 'Come now, Dr Tyrell,' she said lightly. 'I'm here to work, not to evoke remarks like that.'

Matthew leaned closer towards her. 'You're still looking lovely,' he whispered. 'I think I'll have that put on the agenda, we could use a little light relief at these meetings.'

Adele laughed readily. Matthew was being quite flippant for him.

'I'm sure the boss would delete such an item,' she returned.

'Matthew,' a stern voice interrupted. 'We're ready to go in.'

Adele glanced briefly towards the owner of the command, and Matthew gave her a significant squeeze so that they laughed compatibly. Gavin's face was devoid of its earlier good humour. Matthew turned to follow his colleagues, and Adele went on to spend the next hour or so working with Denise, tidying the consulting rooms and restocking them with the doctor's necessary requirements.

As there were no clients visiting that morning on account of the conference there was a more relaxed atmosphere, and the girls had time to chat as they worked.

When Dr Forbes rang through for coffee, Sheila was engrossed in a long conversation with her husband on an outside line, and the other girls elected that it should be Adele who should have the privilege of serving the doctors their mid-morning beverage.

'There's a large tin of assorted biscuits for occasions like this,' Denise explained. 'Demerara sugar, cream—for the favoured few. Butter them up in case anyone's got a complaint against one of us.'

'That sounds ominous,' Adele said.

'Well occasionally you get a personality clash—a client who takes offence at something that normally would go unnoticed. Sometimes people are nervous to the point of being unreasonable, but it is very rare. It is possible at such a quarterly meeting as this, they decide on some change, so we might all be summoned to the board room before the meeting breaks up. Dr Forbes is very fair. If he has any such propositions which affect us, and working conditions, he gets us all together and lets us air our views.'

'I think the clinic is very efficiently run. I wouldn't have thought there was much room for change.'

'I came soon after it opened so there were a few routine changes at the beginning, but our Dr Forbes knows what he wants, and he is a good organiser,' Denise agreed.

The cups and saucers were set out on a tray and the coffee steaming in a large glass coffee pot.

'It's not fair to send you into the wolves on your own,' Denise decided. 'I'll come in and help.'

Adele carried the tray, Denise led the way with the coffee pot.

The men were still engrossed in discussion so appeared to ignore the girls apart from acknowledging being served, Gavin with only a curt nod until leaving the tray and remainder of the coffee on a side table Denise indicated that they could leave, but at the door Gavin halted them.

'All right, Denise, thank you—Adele would you remain a moment please?' he requested.

Adele groaned inwardly. What could she have done wrong? Denise made her exit quickly and left Adele to face the music alone.

Matthew shot her a sympathetic look, or was there a wicked twinkle in his eye? But one glance at Gavin Forbes sitting arrogantly at the head of the table, and she feared the worse by the dark frown on his face.

'A little matter on the agenda which concerns you, Adele,' he said formally, then with a smirk, 'other, that is, than the fact that Dr Tyrell wished to place on record that you're looking particularly lovely this morning—' At this there was a general murmur of approval, and some encouraging twitters of amusement, but Gavin remained straight-faced. 'When you came to us over a month ago you intimated to me that you were going to "give us a try".' The sarcastic comment caused an embarrassing silence.

Adele's nerves were jangling.

'May I ask you what conclusions you've drawn from your trial period?' he asked pertinently.

Adele's mouth had suddenly gone horribly dry. Was he doing this deliberately to make a fool of her? Was it his way of counter-reacting to the affinitive bond between herself and Matthew which Gavin had witnessed, and obviously disapproved.

She shifted one foot nervously, putting all her weight on the other one.

'Now that I've settled down I'm very happy here,' she said softly.

She noticed a slight pucker of his damnably inviting lips, but his gaze was unflinching.

'We were worthy of being given a try?' he pursued scathingly.

Growing familiarity of the room and its occupants gave her some much needed courage.

'I never intended to imply that I was giving *you* a try,' she said boldly. How awful that sounded, but once the words were out she couldn't retract them. 'I mean,' she went on hurriedly, 'I expect it was the other way round, what I meant was, that I had to try to adjust to a rather different daily routine.'

Gavin continued to regard her with a disdainful look.

'You seem to have adjusted admirably, Adele,' he said stiffly. 'Now is the time you have to make the decision though. I seem to remember that you were rather anxious to leave us at one point.'

'I hadn't given myself time—' she began.

'So it was as well that I insist you stay. I was right, after all, wasn't I, Adele?'

'Yes—of course,' she answered with an echo of his own sarcasm, then under her breath added: 'As always.'

His eyelids fluttered angrily denoting that he had heard, and if he had, so had the other members of such distinguished company.

Adele's cheeks were rosy, her eyes full of militancy, but Gavin carried on, choosing to ignore it.

'I'm sure you'll be pleased to know that we've had very good reports from the clients you've dealt with. I'm not going to actually tell you what they said, we can't have you getting too big for your boots.' The emphasis on the last four words brought a response from the others of more twitters. Adele couldn't bear to look at any of them, not even Matthew. She had managed to challenge Gavin up to now by meeting his direct stare, but gradually she was

withering, and now she gulped, her gaze lowered to somewhere on the table, noticing his slender hands resting on the
pad in front of him. 'My colleagues here have also given
their whole-hearted approval and recommendation so I
trust that you have decided to stay?'

'I'd like to very much—thank you, Dr Forbes,' she
managed to say with what she hoped was the right amount
of humility and gratitude.

He smiled then, a self-assured even triumphant smile.

'Good, perhaps you'd come to my office just before you
leave at lunch time, and we'll go through our terms of
agreement.'

It wasn't a question but a command. Adele turned to go
resisting the urge to remind him that she had Oliver to pick
up.

'On the carpet?' Sheila asked when she returned to the
lounge. Was there a hopeful implication in her voice?'

'No,' Adele replied evasively, 'just confirming that I'm
here to stay.'

The other girls congratulated her and showed their pleasure, but Adele sensed that Sheila was on her guard. Up to
now she had enjoyed a good working relationship with all
her colleagues, but today Adele felt uneasy at Sheila's
attitude. It was her imagination she consoled herself as she
continued with the morning's work.

At noon voices in the distance suggested that the conference had ended. At least in the board room, no doubt the
discussion would continue over drinks or lunch which was
where Adele presumed they were going. She was working
in one of the consulting rooms which overlooked the main
street and as she filed away some notes in the cabinet she
looked out of the window to see the group of doctors going
into the hotel opposite. One or two of them were sheltering
beneath umbrellas which they shook vigorously before
going through the revolving door. There was no sign of
Gavin, but then an agile figure sprinted across the road. He
looked so long-legged, so young, and he half-turned his
head away from the wind, his hair already dishevelled. You
could tell him a mile off, Adele thought, by the colour of his

hair. Darker now because it was probably damp, but still golden. At the door of the hotel he paused and glanced back and up to the windows of the clinic. He couldn't possibly see her peeping from the heavy net drapes, but she let the corner fall guiltily and resumed her work.

Just before one o'clock when everyone was preparing to leave Adele began to worry. It was still raining and Jonathan's mother would expect her to pick up the boys. Did she just leave on time and ignore Gavin's request to see him before she left, or did he expect her to wait?

'If he said he'd see you before he left then he'll be back,' Denise said.

'I should go on quickly while you have the chance,' Sheila advised. 'It isn't that important. He can see you tomorrow. I'll explain to him that you had the children to collect.'

But Adele came to a quick decision. 'No, it's okay. I can ring Jonathan's mum. I hadn't better leave without seeing Dr Forbes, he was definite about it.'

Sheila shrugged. 'Suit yourself—I may as well go then. No point in all of us hanging around. You know what men are once they start drinking.'

Adele went to reception and used the telephone there. Jonathan's father was home with a firm's van so offered to go to nursery school to fetch the boys.

'I'm not going to stay for ever,' Adele said to Katy. 'How long do the drinking sessions go on for?'

'I'd be surprised if they are drinking. Wine with a meal perhaps, but if Dr Forbes asked you to wait, he'll be here at one.'

The rest of the girls donned raincoats and left.

'There's no point in me waiting if you're going to be here, so see you tomorrow, Adele,' Katy said.

Adele heard the lift arrive, then Katy's voice and a man's and she turned as Gavin hurried across reception.

'I expected to find you gone—Oliver?' he questioned, dominantly.

'It's all right. Jonathan's father is picking them up—but you're soaked,' she added looking at his wet face and damp jacket.

He held open an arm, indicating her to follow him.

'A drop of rain won't hurt me, Come along—it was good of you to wait.'

In his usual business-like way he went straight to a drawer at his desk and took out a sheaf of papers which he placed on the blotter.

'Come and sit down in the hot seat, fair damsel—you can be perusing your agreement while I dry off.'

He gallantly held his chair while she took her place at the desk.

'Better read it carefully,' he joked, 'make sure I haven't included terms you don't approve of.'

After a moment or two she glanced across at him at the wash basin in one corner where he was vigorously rubbing his hair with a towel. He had removed his dark blue jacket and she couldn't help noticing how the sky blue shirt and matching patterned tie suited him.

With his mass of hair tousled he looked little more than a teenager. His shoulders were broad, but his waist and hips slim, so much virility evident by every quick action.

He turned and she hastily began to read, but she was aware only of him. Without looking up she knew that he was styling his hair into natural attractive waves as he casually strolled over to stand by her side. Surely he must hear her heart thudding?—what could she do to quieten it? The words were just black printed letters, dozens of them, following one after another, completely unreadable through the mist of excitement which had engulfed her. She tried to calm herself, remonstrated with her emotions to keep still, but she could feel his warmth, the power of his sexuality tempting her.

'Something puzzling you, or are you a slow reader as well as a spidery writer?' he teased.

'Do I have to read it now?' she asked, knowing that she simply wasn't capable of comprehending the words.

'Just skim it through enough to sign it—you can read it more thoroughly when you get home if you like.'

'Why the hurry?' Adele attempted to sound nonchalant.

He flung the towel on to the desk, his other hand on her

back, warm but moist through her thin shirt-blouse. With fluttering eyelids she dared to glance up at him. The magic was back. His hand was at her neck sending shivers down her spine. He held her head back and his lips came upon hers with such consuming passion that she began to struggle frantically. She felt so guilty knowing that she wanted this to happen, aware of how she had mentally invited him to touch her, caress her, and then when he did respond she felt afraid—afraid of the wildness of her own capacity for flirting, for that was all it was, her brain hammered home.

Gavin reacted almost like an animal to her struggles and savagely pulled her to her feet.

'Don't think you can play games with me, fair damsel,' he warned, clasping her into his embrace, the fingers of one hand tangling with her hair as he held her fast, his mouth exploring every contour of her face and neck until she was senseless.

'Your dark eyes have been seducing me all morning so now I expect your signature in return,' he chided.

'Isn't that mixing business with pleasure?' she muttered, still at odds with her own wanton desire. 'Is this how you get all your staff to sign an agreement?'

She could feel his muscles hard and powerful against her weakening body. Already his mouth was probing into the opening of the neck of her blouse, and her fingers were gentle at the back of his head, softly persuasive among his damp hair.

With a swift aggressive movement he caught her two hands and pulled them away from his head, forward to his chest where he clutched them painfully in his own strong grip.

'This is lunch time, we're both off duty,' he reminded her. 'Did you really enjoy having your face slapped so much that you're provoking me into repeating such an ungentle-manly action? All right, so no one else is worthy of being called a husband, there's no man on earth who has the fine qualities which Bernie had, but stop accusing me of pulling every female I come into contact with. As Matthew said, you were looking particularly lovely this morning. Why, I wonder? Because over this weekend I've done things which remind you you're a woman—done things which subconsciously you've wanted Matthew to do.'

'What a despicable thing to say,' she flung at him, still breathless from the close contact, hating him for the things he was saying because they weren't true. Not about Matthew, and deep down she despised herself because she had fallen into his trap—he had aroused those inner desires that she had deliberately refused to acknowledge. She was every inch a woman, young and sexually eager even though she had tried to suppress her body's needs. In doing so, and to make her guilt less apparent she turned the tables on this man who was wooing her out of her grief. Some men would have been flattered to be considered a philanderer, but from the intense glare of Gavin's green eyes she knew that she had angered him again.

He pushed her away roughly, picked up the foolscap sheets of paper and thrust them against her heaving breasts cruelly.

'Please your bloody self whether you sign or not,' he said coarsely and turned his back on her as if he couldn't bear to look at her.

She longed to run her hands up his back, to feel the warmth and love emanating from his body, to rest her flushed cheeks against the cool cotton of his shirt. She wanted love—so desperately, but love was the one thing he wasn't offering.

'I really thought that at last we were getting it together,' he said dispassionately. 'You can't go on expecting sympathy for ever, Adele.'

'And you can't expect me to forget Bernie just because you try to show my body what its physical functions are,' she replied with pain in her voice. 'I am human you know.'

He turned again to face her sharply. Drawing out the hurt and suffering by his condemning look.

'I . . . I simply want you to . . . to *feel* again, Adele,' he said, and walked to open the door for her.

Still clutching the terms of agreement she walked blindly out to reception to fetch her coat and bag. She had deluded herself into thinking that every contact, every word had some hidden indication that he was growing fond of her. All the time it was his pattern of therapy, trying to make her aware of other people, helping her to realise that nothing would bring Bernie back. However perfect their love and union had been she must learn to settle for a new set of perfections, a different kind of approach.

Gavin closed the door against her without even saying goodbye. She walked to the lift mechanically, wanting to go, yet willing him to call her back. She couldn't seem to hurry and by the time she reached her car was wet through, but at least the rain mingled with the tears which poured down her cheeks, so that no one was aware of her distress.

For several minutes she sat in the car, drying her face, hands, and her mud-splattered legs with some tissues. Her whole being was left with an emptiness, a shattering anticlimax after the fantasy of anticipation and excitement which she had built up in her mind between Gavin Forbes and herself. He was a ladies' man without doubt, and a man who saw himself as the great healer of all kinds of ills, physical, spiritual, mental—but he had only succeeded in making her pain more tortuous.

That evening she read the generous agreement, and signed it ready to return the next day. It would have been so easy to leave at that point, but no-one else knew what had passed between them, and she didn't intend to give him the satisfaction of seeing her cowardice.

The next day it was as if nothing had happened. Adele made a point of taking the agreement to him personally. He glanced briefly at her signature on both copies, signed them himself and handed hers back to her.

'Good,' he said, and turned his attention to something else on his desk, politely dismissing her.

But as the days passed she could not dismiss from her mind the response she had felt at his advances. She kept telling herself that he had been kind to her and Oliver, that it meant no more than that. There was Vivien, after all, and soon she was going to be living at Beecroft. It was going to be unbearable knowing that Gavin was under the same roof, visiting Viv, doing all the things that Adele would love to share with him.

Love was such an unbidden emotion. It came to taunt, bringing anguish and joy in turn, but Adele did her best to hide her sentiments.

Gavin seemed to deliberately avoid noticing her, but on occasion would suddenly meet her gaze with acute intensity thus causing her to come out of her daydreams and avert her eyes. She tried to discipline herself to behave normally when in his company, but the feeling of impending magic was ever present.

The prospect of going to the country with him held her in awe. She wondered if he would change the arrangement, but he made reference to it several times, and a few days before told her at what time he would be calling to pick them up. Adele knew she was a fool, but she looked forward to simply being with him even if there were to be no thrills. She must admire him from afar. At least he hadn't let Oliver down. He had crossed off each day on the calendar with great enthusiasm and at last the day arrived, and after the morning's work Adele fetched Oliver from nursery school. He remained glued to the lounge window waiting for Uncle Gavin, who arrived while Adele was putting the final touches to the small flat Vivien was to occupy. She had bought a small fern and a begonia to place on the window-sill, and a vase of chrysanthemums from the garden stood in the centre of the small drop-leaf table.

'It looks very inviting, fair damsel.' The voice from the doorway surprised her. She had been thinking of the numerous times when she had wished she had not been persuaded to let Vivien have the flat, but since it was all freshened up she realised it needed to be lived in.

'I hope Vivien will be happy here,' Adele said, flushing slightly at being caught rearranging the flowers. 'It is very small.'

'Compact is the word I would choose, Adele. A small place is easy to heat, and more cosy for one person. I think Viv is very fortunate—and you know, of course, that if circumstances alter, or you just don't want her here, you have only to say.'

'That does sound heartless,' Adele said.

'Better to be honest, relationships can become strained, even among friends,' he said pointedly.

As she came out on to the landing, closing the flat door, Gavin flicked her shoulder-length hair in a playful gesture. She remembered how she had shrunk from his brush on that first morning at *A Votre Santé* clinic. Little had she thought then how differently she would come to feel about Gavin Forbes.

'I've left the central heating on a low setting so it will all keep aired and warm ready for our return on Sunday,' she explained as they went downstairs.

'Don't talk about coming back, Adele, we haven't set off yet—but—' he added laughing, 'it looks as if we're about to. Young Oliver has struggled out with your cases.'

'*I'm* ready,' Oliver announced, re-appearing in the hall, his cheeks rosy and plump to match the glow of his warm red trousers and his red and yellow fair-isle bobble hat covering up his dark curly hair. A smart leather belted jacket completed his outfit in readiness for the journey farther north than the midlands town in which they lived.

Adele experienced a moment's panic as they left the busy city behind. It was her first trip away since Bernie's death—her first night away from her own bed—just herself and Oliver. Even the packing had seemed significant, but as they drove along the motorway and then into peaceful rural districts she relaxed and on reaching Cedar Grove, a splendid country house set in cedar tree parkland, she was greeted so warmly that all apprehension vanished.

The size of Honey, and her exuberance at seeing her master overwhelmed Oliver at first, but he soon got used to the dog again and wouldn't be parted from her.

In a huge comfortable lounge they sat round a blazing log fire to enjoy afternoon tea, after which Gavin showed Adele to her room. It was one of about six double bedrooms, and Oliver was to occupy a small single room which connected with Gavin's.

'I decided being in a strange place he might like to know he was within easy reach of me,' Gavin said.

Adele felt momentarily put out. Gavin Forbes was really quite obnoxious at times, surely he realised that children were likely to need their mothers when in unfamiliar surroundings?

'I want you to have a complete rest, fair damsel,' he went on, reading her mind. 'He knows you're right next door on the opposite side, but he thought it was fun being in my dressing room.'

'He could have been in with me, Gavin,' Adele said. 'I hope your mother hasn't gone to any trouble.'

'Oh she has,' he said, throwing a mock punch towards her chin, 'but you and Oliver, my darling, are worth it—I hope.'

He talked in riddles, was frequently teasing, so that she wasn't always sure how to take him.

He guided her to the window, pointing out the extent of his mother's land. The countryside looked bleak, but less dismal than the city had done, and she was already drawn to exploring the vast acreage as she peered through the double-glazing, Gavin standing behind her, his face nuzzling in her hair and his hands linked across the front of her.

'I can't undo my case, Mummy,' Oliver said, coming in through the open doorway.

'It's not locked, darling,' Adele said, escaping Gavin's imprisonment. 'But, of course, you don't like the spring fastening, I'll come and unpack your things.'

'We eat at about seven, Adele—can Oliver stay up?'

'Oh yes please, Mummy—say yes—can I?'

'You didn't have a nap today though after lunch, did you?' Adele reminded him.

'No, but I will be good,' he promised.

He was, and Adele felt justifiably proud of Oliver's behaviour at dinner, and afterwards he went to bed with no fuss and was quickly asleep.

The atmosphere was homely and relaxing, and Adele felt contented. Vivien was looking better than when Adele had seen her last and she showed her eagerness at going to live at Beecroft.

'I'm afraid it's rather small,' Adele refreshed Vivien's memory. 'You'll miss all this spacious living.'

'My rooms in London were large but dreary,' Vivien said. 'I shall love Beecroft—I know I shall. I'm so grateful to you, Adele.'

'I haven't shown you around yet, fair damsel, have I?' Gavin intervened and taking her hand in his led her out of the lounge. The rest of the house was equally warm and comfortable. They started at the top, looking in on Oliver who looked happy in his dreams. Gavin's room was large and overlooked the driveway as did two more elegant bedrooms, while Mrs Lascelles' and Vivien's were on the south side. There were two well-equipped bathrooms and a shower room on a lower landing.

The dining room where they had eaten dinner was huge and furnished in Jacobean style, opening into a lean-to greenhouse.

On the west side of the front entrance Gavin opened the door of a room which was clearly a study. He paused and waited while Adele took in the style of room it was and then he smiled as she gasped.

'A consulting room—you've practised here?' she asked.

'No—my step-father was the country doctor here for several years after his father before him.'

'Is that why you went into medicine?'

Gavin shrugged. 'I suppose so—I was hardly out of medical school when my step-father died so not qualified enough to take over the practice here. Lassie wanted to keep on this house for Vivien's sake so a new doctor took over in the next village, but Lassie likes to keep this room as it was.'

'It's a wonderful house,' Adele said with feeling.

'They only had seven years together, but they did lots of modernisation to the place in that time—come and see the swimming pool.'

He led her through the hall to a door down at the end of a passageway near the kitchen.

'This was all out-houses—my step-father kept the existing walls, but had the interior ones knocked down and the whole area made into an indoor heated swimming pool.'

'How splendid—it's in use all the year round?'

'That's right. Lassie swims every day—she found she was getting signs of arthritis even in her younger days, that's why John, my stepfather, decided on this.'

'How sad, Gavin, to lose two husbands so tragically.'

'Yes, indeed. My step-father was a fine man—a really dedicated doctor and a wonderful personality. It was tragic that he died when only in his fifties. He worked himself to death, I'm afraid.'

They walked around the edge of the pool as he showed her the changing rooms and toilets.

'Tomorrow you must start the day with a swim,' Gavin said.

'You didn't tell me to bring a swimsuit,' she replied with disappointment.

Gavin only laughed. 'We don't let little things like that worry us. It *is* heated, and you can have the place to yourself—well, you could, but—'

Adele chose not to pursue the matter, but wondered what the 'but' might have led to.

She loved everything about the 'Olde worlde' charm of Cedar Grove and after a good night's rest followed by breakfast on a tray brought to her by Gavin she got up and with Oliver explored the grounds.

Overnight it had turned much colder and there was still some sparkling frost covering the fields and grass as Gavin showed them the little grotto at the lower end of the grounds, the small lake where wild birds came back year after year, and they returned through the copse, coming to the cedar grove where Gavin and Oliver kicked a ball about before lunch.

Their cheeks were glowing, and their appetites aroused and eager for the delicious hot soup Lassie served. Lunch was a substantial meal and lasted nearly two hours, during which the conversation covered many subjects.

When Adele had finished her coffee she excused herself and Oliver.

'I expect it will be best for everyone if he had his usual nap,' she said, and after settling him, with Honey in her basket on the landing outside Gavin's door, Adele returned to the dining room, surprised to find Gavin alone.

'Another cup of coffee, Adele?' he asked.

'Mm—yes, I would like one, please—then I can wash up.'

'You won't, my girl, I brought you here for a holiday weekend. Besides, Mother has her daily to help her. She always has a rest for a couple of hours after lunch, and Viv too since her operation, so—you come with me.'

He stood waiting by her chair until she had drunk her coffee, then he clasped her hand tightly and took her along to the swimming pool. She gasped when she heard the click of the key in the lock.

'Now don't start protesting, fair damsel—just get in there and get your clothes off. You think nothing of wandering about at the club with nothing on, so just forget I'm here.' Before Adele could think up excuses he went on: 'And you needn't pretend you're cold—it's almost too hot in here. I put the thermostat up especially for you. Don't forget I did come to your aid in the sauna. That's the next thing I want to instal here for Lassie, but we have to get Viv established first.'

He was already undoing his tie as he went into one cubicle. Adele hesitated and he put his head round the door.

'Now you can do it the easy way, fair damsel, or I can throw you in—makes no difference to me either way.'

'You're impossible,' Adele said. 'What about Oliver?'

'Oliver is fast asleep and Viv will hear him if he wakes. He might like to come in too—now, don't tell me you're that old-fashioned. This is supposed to be the modern eighties.'

'Well I don't happen to be that permissive,' she argued.

He pulled his trousers off and Adele quickly disappeared into the next cubicle.

She could keep her briefs and bra on—but, oh what the heck, she thought as she heard an echoing splash, and was quick to follow suit.

The water was sensuously warm and she enjoyed swimming the length of the pool and back again. Gavin discreetly left her alone for a while, but then he swam up to her, pulled her back against him and swam with her floating above him. They swam together, ducked and dived in childish play and after he had kissed her violently she doggy-paddled back to get her breath, and as he stood up in the pool she noticed that his body was a mass of rich golden hair.

Her body was awake to the influence their nakedness aroused. She couldn't hide the thrill she experienced as her limbs floated gently in the water, then she turned and swam away from him, knowing that he would chase and tantalise, until breathless and crazy with desire he pulled her out after him and running to the far end of the pool drew her into his arms as he switched on the shower.

'My mother and step-father were very much in love,' he whispered. 'Only one shower down here—but you know how passionate the French are reputed to be.'

He soaped his hands, and she was hungry for his gentle touch over her breasts, her arms, her back, running through her hair. In spite of the soap in them she tried to keep her eyes open intrigued by the firm muscles of the man who held her close, tenderly, expertly reminding her of his needs, and of the needs of a woman in love . . .

CHAPTER EIGHT

THE icy coldness of the change in temperature made Adele shriek and try to get out of Gavin's clutches.

'You beast,' she yelled. 'You unfeeling swine.'

He held her face upwards to take the softened cold water as it sprayed over them and his mouth covered hers in yet an ever more demanding kiss. But the coolness of the water over the rest of their bodies, rinsing off the soap suds, succeeded in calming their impassioned emotions.

'I hope I haven't ruined a costly hair-do', Gavin said as she let the water rinse the soap out of her hair.

'No, I do it myself,' she answered back between gasps.

He switched off the water and left her briefly, to return dressed in a towelling robe, and he placed another one round Adele's shoulders—a sort of cape which tied at the neck. He rubbed her vigorously and then with their clothes over their arms they crept back through the slumbering house and upstairs.

Adele put her clothes on the bed and quietly went to look in on Oliver who was sleeping soundly.

Gavin came through the connecting doorway from his room, rubbing his hair with a small towel. She smiled at him, unashamed this time at the admiration which must exude from her gaze. He took her hand in his and pulled her away from Oliver's bedside, into his own bedroom.

The curtains were partially drawn for Oliver's benefit, the bed covers rolled back. He made his way towards the bed with Adele hesitantly following. She couldn't speak—she wanted him so much, yet she knew that it was too soon, and not permissible with Oliver in the adjoining room.

Gavin's eyes seemed the deeper turquoise blue for the love and passion which was reflected in them.

'No, Gavin,' she whispered huskily, pulling back.

With lips that almost touched hers he whispered: 'A nap

will do you good, darling.' He pulled her down on the bed beside him. 'I want to make love to you, but I'm not so thoughtless that I would wish to waken or upset Oliver. When I make love to you, fair damsel it will be when we can be entirely alone. My desire is such for you that I want to hear your squeals of delight, your pleas for more—there will be no room for inhibitions.'

Gently he moved her legs round so that she was lying in the crook of his arm. He kissed her eyelids closed and then she felt the tender movement of his fingers untying the cord at her neck. She felt her body contract. What was the use of saying no when he still carried on as he wanted to do.

'Oliver might wake,' she muttered, opening her eyes.

'If he does I shall go to him. If you're asleep I shall let you sleep on—if you're awake you can slip out of my door and go to your own room to dress. I'll take Oliver downstairs and give him one of those enormous ice-creams from the freezer.'

'You spoil him outrageously,' she admonished in a hushed tone.

'In a different way from smothering him with mother-love,' he answered in a low voice. 'But while we have time just let me love you my way.'

His gaze moved slowly downwards from her face as he lifted back the edges of the robe. He kissed her satin-smooth neck, then sliding his sensuous lips over her body he caressed her to sleep.

If Adele had opened her eyes before drifting into the security of a deep sleep she would have seen Gavin surveying her body not only with desire but with a glimmer of amusement. He was glad she didn't open her eyes. He didn't want to be the one to tell her that there was considerably more flesh on her bones now than when he had first met her . . .

When Adele woke about an hour later she stretched and felt a pang of disappointment at finding the bed empty. The sheets and blankets were tucked all round her, the damp robe having been removed. How had he managed that, she wondered, without waking her. She stretched again and ran her fingers lightly over her skin, remembering Gavin's kisses. She felt deliciously contented until her thoughts moved on to the other occupants of the house. Mrs Lascelles had made her and Oliver so welcome; Vivien too on the surface seemed pleasant enough, but what was there between her and Gavin? Over this weekend Adele hoped to find out.

At length she pushed back the covers and sat on the side of the bed wondering how she could get to her own room without meeting anyone. She stood up and walked across to the long mirror, seeing the same naked body which Gavin had looked at with such affection. Not such a bad figure now, she decided with a wry smile, but as Matthew had said she didn't really want to get plump again. She poked her fingers into her flesh, but met firm muscle and had to admit that she was in a better condition after her sessions at the gym.

A man's silk dressing-gown lay over the chair, put there she suspected by Gavin, who did seem to think of everything. She slipped it on and tiptoed back to her own room, listening for the sound of anyone else, but the house was quiet.

She brushed her honey-coloured hair until it fell in soft waves down to her shoulders, then she cleaned her teeth and rubbed moisturising cream all over her body before dressing in a purple two-piece, skirt and long waistcoat, under which she wore a white jumper.

She felt invigorated as she walked down the wide oak staircase and almost wished she could go for another swim.

Mrs Lascelles was sitting by the fire, sipping tea from a small white bone-china cup.

'Ah—Adele, *chérie*, come and have tea wis me.'

'Where is everyone?' Adele asked.

'I sink Gavin will have taken Oliver and Honey out for a walk while it is still light. Tell me—have you slept?'

'Yes, I'm afraid I did.'

'Why be afraid?—it will do you good—and the change of air. I am getting old and find now that a rest after lunch is necessary.'

'You don't look old, Lassie—really, not a day over forty-five.'

'Because, Adele, I try to keep young for Gavin. He also I think looks younger than his thirty-seven years, yes? Despite all the un'appiness in his life he tries to be light-hearted. He says other people don't want to know about his sadness. I know this too. When my first husband died I thought I could not go on living. People were kind, but what could they do? They could not bring Guy back, but I expected them to be sad too. I lived for Gavin—just as your whole life now is Oliver—but, my dear, you must live a life for yourself too.'

Adele sipped the tea, finding it refreshing after her nap, but her astute brain was keen to probe into Gavin's past.

'Gavin has never married,' she remarked casually.

Mrs Lascelles looked intently at Adele.

'Married!' she repeated. 'Did you not know that he was within six weeks of being married when his fiancée, Anita, became ill? The wedding was postponed, but she died of cancer, a rare and dreadful kind. He hides his heartache well, but he suffers, Adele, oh how he grieves.'

'I . . . I'm so sorry, I didn't know.'

'That is typical of Gavin, he would not wish his colleagues even to know. That is why he decided to start the clinic—in memory of his father, his step-father, his fiancée.'

'How long ago?' Adele dared to enquire.

'Nearly three years, and only just this past few months does he seem to laugh again. Your son, Adele, has brought him such joy. He loves children and worked with them until this last tragedy. He would make a fine father—I hope,' Lassie sighed, 'perhaps he and Vivien—they are fond of each other, but has she got over Jacques yet, I ask myself?'

'Jacques? Her business partner?'

'That is right. Gavin's cousin. Jacques and Gavin are good friends too. Jacques is in the designing trade also, so Gavin took Vivien to France when she left college and she fell in love with Jacques. They have been together a long time, but now the business goes on, but not the romance.'

Lassie laughed. 'That is the strange ways of men and women—but I would like to see her happy.' She sighed deeply. 'Both of them, I want only the best,' she added.

Adele's spirits sagged. She had felt so free and happy with Gavin. Did Lassie know how she had just put a damper on her new-found happiness?

She took a small cake which Lassie offered not because she wanted one, but because she hoped it might hide her sadness. The news of Gavin having been engaged had come as a shock. She realised now that he had befriended her and Oliver because he had experienced a tragic loss also, but now Lassie had voiced her worst fears that there was something between Gavin and Vivien. It sounded as if Lassie were doing everything to encourage them. What would she think if she knew Gavin had come close to making love to her? Swimming naked in the pool, lying together on his bed? Adele was sure she loved Gavin sincerely. There were times when she hated him, but that was the real test of love—to go on loving in spite of his faults. But from now on she must not respond to his philandering.

'Ah, here they come, I can hear Honey barking,' Lassie said, getting up and going over to the window. Adele went to join her and saw Gavin and Oliver playing hide-and-seek among the trees—but she also saw a third party strolling along behind them—it was Vivien.

Adele felt every nerve tighten and as if Lassie had felt her reaction she placed an arm round Adele's waist.

'He is a charming little boy, *ma chérie*,' she said. 'I know how you feel—I too felt that I must be everything to Gavin—both mother and father. It is a difficult task to bring up a child alone—I had Guy's parents—but your own parents are in Canada and you have no one. Don't neglect your own desires, Adele, for Oliver. He will grow up and the years pass by so quickly, and it is bad for a boy to consider his *maman* first.'

'Did Gavin grow possessive over you?' Adele asked gently.

Lassie sighed. 'There were signs of it—and too late I saw

my mistake. The Forbes family saw it also—they too doted on him, so I had to take a decision I did not like, and sent him away to school. It broke my heart, but we both had to learn to do wi'sout ze other.'

Lassie tapped the window and Oliver came running towards the french doors. While Adele waited and watched she saw Gavin turn to Vivien and hold out his hand to her. For a second they were hidden behind a tree and when they emerged they had their arms about one another. Did they steal a quick kiss behind the cedar tree?

Honey bounded into the lounge ahead of Oliver who came laughing and breathless up to the doorway.

'Don't come in, Oliver,' Adele warned, 'your wellies are all muddy.'

'And Honey's paws,' Lassie said. 'Now—stay. I will fetch the old towel,' she directed.

Oliver hung on to Adele's neck while she pulled off his boots.

'Have you had a lovely time, darling?' she asked.

'Talking to me?' Gavin said in a sly undertone, patting the top of her head as they came up behind Oliver. 'Had fun, haven't we, Oliver? While your Mummy was a lazy girl and slept.'

Adele didn't look up at Gavin—how could she when her heart was so weak with longing for him?

'Let's go and find your slippers,' she said to Oliver, 'and you need a wash too, I expect.'

Lassie passed an old towel to Gavin who cleaned Honey's paws much to Oliver's amusement and then Adele took Oliver upstairs.

Vivien followed them. 'Did you have a good rest, Adele?' she asked.

'Yes, I dropped off I'm afraid,' Adele said lightly. 'I mustn't get into those habits at my age.'

'You look younger every time I see you—that's a good sign,' Vivien said. 'Why shouldn't you have a daytime rest if you feel better for it? That young man keeps you on the go I'm sure.'

'That's good for her,' Gavin said, reaching the landing in

long two-at-a-time strides. 'What did you do with all the things you collected for Mummy, Oliver?'

'In my pocket.' He pulled out leaves, twigs, grasses and fircones.

'I expect you'd like to take them to school on Monday,' she said.

'No—I brought them for you,' and he placed his grubby hands around her neck and hugged Adele tightly.

She felt dishevelled and flushed when she disentangled herself from his arms.

'I think you'd better come and wash your hands, darling,' she said, aware that Gavin was watching them closely.

Vivien had gone on to her own room and as Oliver ran to the bathroom Gavin restrained Adele.

'A good sleep?' he whispered.

Adele nodded, trying to appear indifferent, but meeting his gaze she just couldn't help showing her affection for him. 'I'm being spoiled,' she said. 'I mustn't make a habit of sleeping during the day or I shan't sleep at night.'

Gavin raised his eyebrows, but made no comment as he went into his own room.

When Adele went to Oliver's room to help him change his clothes Gavin had discreetly closed the communicating door, and Adele tried to keep Oliver from talking too loudly. Then they went downstairs to the lounge where Lassie had made a fresh pot of tea, and toasted a plateful of crumpets.

Oliver sat on Adele's lap close to the fire and when Gavin returned soon afterwards—Adele had been torturing herself with thoughts of passionate scenes taking place upstairs between Gavin and Vivien—he looked immaculate in a dark brown suit, cream shirt and colourful orange and brown tie, and her heart turned a somersault in admiration. In her mind's eye she could visualise his firm body covered with golden curls which lay hidden beneath shirt and waistcoat. The cosiness of sharing afternoon tea with Gavin and his family helped her to overcome her crazy desire for her boss. Was it because Vivien seemed to mean something special to him that she wanted him? Occasionally their glances met and always she saw that gleam in his; a hint of mischief, a well of sensuality.

As they had eaten a substantial lunch and now enjoyed afternoon tea refreshments it was decided that as no one was hungry they would turn dinner into a later but light supper. Television was switched on for a suitable programme for Oliver and then Adele suggested it was bedtime.

'I stayed up last night,' he said with a pout.

'That was a special occasion,' Adele explained.

'But . . . but, if I go to bed I . . . I won't see Honey.'

'Tomorrow, darling,' Adele tried to pacify, but she knew by the determination in the set of his mouth, and his large brown eyes, so much like her own, that he was ready to put up a fight.

This was what she dreaded, a confrontation in front of strangers, and in someone else's house.

'It's bedtime, Oliver, and that's that,' she said firmly.

She watched his lower lip begin to quiver.

'But I won't see Lassie and Uncle Gavin after tomorrow.'

'Another time—of course you will,' she assured him.

'You won't let me,' he said loudly, desperately trying to hide the panic in his voice.

'Why ever not?' Adele asked beginning to laugh.

'Because I . . . I'm going to cry,' he said between sobs, and then he turned on Adele aggressively, punching the top half of her viciously.

'Oliver!' Gavin's stern voice made the little boy pause, and turning to look at the severe doctor Oliver reverted to a tirade of abuse directed at Adele.

She could have excused him on the grounds of being tired. The excitement, the strange surroundings, the accumulation of adults were all a bit too much for him she knew, and wasn't she finding the strain of this unusual weekend herself? But she also knew that she must be firm, so she pushed Oliver away, got up and dragged him to the door.

'Are you going to say goodnight?' she asked.

'No!' he shouted, so she hauled him out of the room and protesting up the stairs.

'I'm ashamed of you, Oliver,' she remonstrated as she

peeled off his clothes angrily. 'You'd been so good up to now. Lassie won't ask you back here again.'

At this he set up a bellow, pleading and begging, but she kissed him goodnight and switched off the light before hurrying to the privacy of her own room.

She supposed Gavin and Matthew would say she was handling it all wrong, but how could Oliver let her down like this? If only Bernie—but she had to discipline Oliver all by herself.

His bellowing was alternated with shrieks and screams, sobbing and calling which she recognised as over-excitement. There was only one way to deal with it and anger took her storming back to his room, pulling the covers off him, down with his pyjama trousers and a good old-fashioned smacked bottom which resounded violently.

'I've had enough, Oliver—now go to sleep at once,' she shouted, and then returned to her own room where she flung herself down on her bed in a fit of uncontrollable weeping. More angry with herself for giving way to her pent-up emotions—which not only included having to control Oliver, but having to control her own combination of judgments. Judgments of her personal feelings for Gavin, judgments of his feelings for her, and Vivien, and knowing that he was right now judging her handling of her young son.

It tore her heart to pieces to listen to Oliver's crying—how she despised herself for using physical punishment, for displaying her own temper thus.

She was thankful to be alone, and then strong hands forced her up from the bed.

'That hurt you much more than it did him,' Gavin said softly. 'Now go to him and make it up,' he commanded gently. 'Dry those tears first though.'

He was trying to make her look at him, but she pulled away, went to the vanity unit and splashed her face with cold water before returning to Oliver's room.

'I can come back—I can, Mummy—please?' Oliver pleaded, becoming convulsed in yet more crying.

'Of course you can, Oliver.' Gavin somehow got to him before Adele, held the tear-stained cheeks between his hands and soothed the distraught Oliver.

'We'll talk about that tomorrow,' Adele intervened. She sat on the side of the bed smoothing Oliver's damp, ruffled hair and put her cheek against his.

'Go to sleep now, darling,' she whispered.

'Where's Honey?' Oliver whimpered.

'In her basket on the landing, but you'll frighten her away if you make that awful noise.' She kissed him several times and then left him, the sound of his childish sobs almost too much for her to bear.

'Please leave me,' she said turning to Gavin who had followed her into her bedroom.

'Certainly not. You're my guest and I don't like to see you upset.'

'I'm sorry Oliver misbehaved,' she said walking round the room in distress. 'I suppose I usually handle him better than that when we're on our own.'

'By giving in to him I suspect,' Gavin chided.

'What would you know about it?' she returned tartly. 'All children are naughty sometimes—especially when you want them to be good.'

'Especially then,' Gavin echoed. 'Darling, I do understand, and I admire you for being firm—a little hard even when probably I'm just as much to blame for getting him too excited. He won't bear a grudge—children never do—they accept it as being all part of growing up. I know how you hate yourself for resorting to being physical—but he'll thank you for that when he grows up. He'll have forgotten it by morning.'

'I doubt that,' she replied bitterly. 'Of course I hate myself.'

'Don't brood over it—listen—he's quiet—I'm sure he'll be fast asleep. Hurry up and get ready.'

'Get ready?' she questioned.

'I'm taking you to a night club.'

'Oh no you're not,' she said adamantly, with bitter contempt in her voice. 'I wouldn't leave Oliver now, and anyway—I—I think I'd rather go to bed myself. Perhaps you'd make my excuses to your mother and Vivien.'

Gavin strode across the room impatient with her fit of belligerence.

'No, I will not. You can't just opt out because Oliver has played up a bit. I've booked a table at the Waverley Hot Spot.'

'You didn't say—if you had asked me I could have told you I didn't wish to go to a night club. Besides, I've got a headache,' she added lamely.

Gavin lifted his hands, part despair, part fury.

'For God's sake, Adele, that's the oldest trick in the book—give me credit for more intelligence than to believe that.'

'*You* don't know how my head feels,' she argued. 'And while we're on the subject, and for the record—you can make what decrees you like in your professional life but not personal ones concerning me. I make my own decisions.'

'In your emotional state you're capable of making the wrong ones, you can use a little help, a little direction, like now for instance—when I'm doing my damndest to take some of the responsibility from your shoulders.'

'Then your intentions are misguided,' she retorted. 'In the first place *I* have decided that I don't go anywhere or with anyone unless Oliver knows about it beforehand and understands. He's *my* responsibility, my top priority twenty-four hours a day, seven days a week. Everything I do now will affect his behaviour in the future—I don't expect *you* to understand—you may be good with children, think you understand them but when you have your own flesh and blood to consider it's a different matter.'

She knew she was wounding him deeply, so deeply that he just stared at her.

'I'm sorry if I've spoilt your plans,' she continued humbly. 'You can take your mother and Vivien.'

'If I had wanted to take them, Adele, I could do it at any time. This was to be your weekend.'

'Well, I'm sorry,' she repeated. 'Surely you could discuss things?—you just take everything upon yourself and force people to go along with you. I object to being taken for granted.'

He was looking downcast and Adele felt full of remorse knowing that she was letting fly at him because she was disappointed in Oliver, as well as the turmoil in herself regarding Gavin.

'I take your point in wanting to tell Oliver of your plans,' he said at length. 'That is sensible, of course, and I apologise for not being more thoughtful; as you so rightly remind me, I don't have my own flesh and blood—but I am willing to learn. All the same I don't consider it was necessary to smack him with quite such vehemence however much his outburst displeased you. There was more than the usual wrath behind that fit of rage.' He paused probably hoping she would enlighten him and when she didn't he turned to the door adding: 'I seem to have erred on the side of over-enthusiasm, so I'll simply telephone the Waverley and cancel my booking.'

'I'm sorry, Gavin,' Adele said, weakening at his humility. 'Really I am. I do appreciate all that you've done for Oliver and me.'

He came back to face her slowly, searching her expression for some sign of her former adulation.

'Then just to please me will you come down to supper?'

'Do I have to?' she whispered.

'You're making the decisions,' he reminded her, then grinning wickedly he said: 'Yes, you do.' He leaned forward and kissed her forehead tenderly. 'We'll do the Waverley another time—but—you can't possibly go to bed yet, it's barely eight-thirty and as you said yourself, after sleeping this afternoon you won't sleep tonight.'

It was inevitable that she didn't. At least not for the first couple of restless hours. Even after a pleasant supper and evening spent cosily round the fire she felt guilty at spoiling Gavin's well-organised weekend. In an effort to make her feel less upset at Oliver's behaviour Lassie had talked about Gavin in his younger days, and then Vivien had eagerly anticipated how things were going to work out at Beecroft and inevitably the subject of Christmas had cropped up.

'Vivien will come here, of course,' Lassie announced.

'And you, Adele, must bring Oliver for a family Christmas.'

'It's very kind of you, but I have already made up my mind to stay at Beecroft,' Adele said. 'I really think children are best in their own homes.'

'But Christmas is a time for children—we should love to have you both here,' Lassie insisted.

'My parents want me to fly over to Canada, but if I do that they'll expect me to settle there—I may do that eventually, but at present I need to take things slowly, and I have no wish to be away from Beecroft for long—besides it's unwise during the winter with freeze-ups and so on.'

She was grateful that they didn't press her further, except to say that the invitation stood if she changed her mind at the last minute.

Lying alone in the dark she hoped she hadn't offended them, but it was true, she did have to tread warily. Time alone would heal the scars Bernie's death had inflicted, and now she had the added dilemma of her feelings for Gavin. But what did that matter, she was forced to ask herself, when he loved Vivien? Whatever he did or said it all came back to the same thing in the end—he was using her for his own purposes, to get Vivien the flat. Because of his own heartache he could feel some sympathy with Adele, but there it ended. She felt sad for Oliver who was besotted with Gavin. For herself she could love the handsome doctor for as long as he showed interest in her, but the time would surely come when he would begin to cool off.

If only Matthew had let her grieve alone, but he had made the suggestion of her working in her best interests and she knew it had worked. Taken her away from Beecroft and all its memories for just a few hours each day and given her a purpose in life. Wasn't it rewarding if just occasionally a patient's tests proved positive in time for treatment and a cure to be effective? A small percentage perhaps, but a life saved in place of Bernie's, another in memory of Gavin's Anita? and there was hope for Vivien. Yes, she was at least involved in something worthwhile.

Sleep at last came in the early hours, a deep, lasting

unconsciousness which healed the bruises of the day, and even when she did wake she turned over and dozed off again with no inclination to face the last few hours at Cedar Grove. For a short while she slept heavily again, being Sunday morning and no sounds of activity to disturb her. Vaguely she wondered whether Oliver was awake or not, and eventually she roused herself sufficiently to get out of bed to look out of the window from which she saw a pale wintry sun glistening on the morning frost.

She looked down at herself, thankful that Lassie's home was well heated As a last-minute crazy idea she had packed an apricot-coloured negligee, with a matching dainty lace-trimmed nightgown. Who did she think she was going to impress, she thought idly? but somehow going to Gavin's home it hadn't seemed right to take brushed nylon night attire, bed-socks and bed-jacket. Her recent comfort as the nights had grown colder had been a hot water bottle for when she had switched off the electric under-blanket, and thankfully here at Cedar Grove she had enjoyed the luxury of a fluffy over-blanket which she could set to any temperature she chose and keep on for as long as she needed it.

She hadn't bothered to look at the time, but when she felt the rush of draught as the door opened she turned expecting to see Oliver, instead Gavin entered carrying a tray of tea and toast. He too had slept late it seemed, for he was wearing a short black and white checked bath-robe, the belt loosely tied so that the front sagged open revealing his masculine chest. She noticed that bare legs and forearms were all covered with the same golden down.

'Good morning, fair damsel,' he greeted. 'I've brought this for you to be going on with as we've decided on brunch today—is that okay?'

'It sounds perfect,' Adele said, with a grateful smile. 'I thought you would be Oliver.'

'Sorry to disappoint you—he's up and out with Lassie and Viv.'

'So early?'

Gavin had placed the tray on a small table near the other window, now he came towards Adele his sparkling green eyes showing his appreciation of her attire. Too late she realised she ought to have hopped smartly back into bed.

'Is five minutes to ten early by your standards?' he asked looking at his watch.

'Heavens—I'm afraid I've lost all track of time.'

'But you eventually slept—that's what is important.' She nodded and he went on: 'I heard you go to the bathroom at midnight and look in on Oliver on your way back. Oliver woke at about seven, so we read a story—'

'You should have woken me, sent him in to me. I'm so sorry you were disturbed.'

'Don't be sorry, darling—we had a great time and then Lassie and Viv decided to take Honey for a walk so naturally Oliver wanted to go too.'

'A lot he cares about his Mum it seems,' Adele said with a laugh.

'He wanted to see you so we crept in and he said sorry with a kiss on your cheek,' Gavin explained softly.

A lump came up in Adele's throat. This maddening individual could always seem to do the right thing. She turned quickly and looked out of the window.

'A heavy frost,' she said croakily.

'Outside—we don't want any frost inside—have you been warm enough?'

'Beautifully warm.' She turned and smiled at Gavin readily. 'At home I've had to resort to woollies and bed-socks and hot water bottles. A big bed is no place to sleep alone in winter.'

'It needs another occupant,' Gavin crooned in her ear as he squeezed her waist. She was eager for his touches again. He nuzzled her neck, nibbled her ear and teased until she was helpless with laughter and as his hands slid down over the front of her she sank back against his firm torso happily.

During the next couple of minutes of uninhibited horse-play Adele lost the negligee, and as his mouth sunk into her shoulders his hands crept up beneath the fine silk of her nightgown. His loving fingertips brushed a sensational path from hip to hip causing Adele to gasp with pleasure as he buried his face in her milk-white skin. He seemed to be devouring her and she closed her eyes, breathless with desire.

God, she thought, how long since her senses had been aroused to such unquenchable depths, but Gavin was quenching her thirst for satisfaction. It couldn't stop now, she thought, as he slid the lace straps of her gown over her shoulders and when it reached her feet he picked it up and threw it on to the bed.

'You're just too lovely not to be loved, darling,' he whispered. She returned his caresses, seeking out the sensitive spots in his body, sliding her fingers through the matt of golden curls until man and woman were caught up together in a frenzy of temptation.

'Oh, Gavin, I love you,' she whispered, 'I love you so much,' and his expert courtship brought an involuntary shudder through her then with a cruel turn of suspension he swept her up and over his shoulder and set off through the house, not releasing her until their bodies sliced through the water in the swimming pool with a huge splash.

The change of mood was a shock to Adele. She came up spluttering and indignant, and he reached her, grasping her waist between determined hands.

'Why?' she asked, her deep brown eyes ablaze with scorn. 'Why must you torment me like this?'

She pressed hard on his hands and he released her, then with a violent overarm stroke he swam to the side, scrambled out of the pool, draped a towel round his waist and disappeared.

Never, ever, had she had dealings with such an insufferable, cruel swine, she declared inaudibly.

The ache in her body was gone. She felt vexed with herself realising that she had probably cheapened herself in Gavin's eyes. She had whispered words of love, words that *she* knew she meant, not merely an idle display of passion lasting for a reckless moment or two, but evidently Gavin's love-making had no genuine motives. Without being aware of what she was doing she was swimming furiously up and down the pool giving vent to her wayward emotions, and the disappointment of yet more empty flirtation.

CHAPTER NINE

It had to stop, she vowed, as under the shower a few minutes later she soaped herself vigorously, almost painfully as if the harsh treatment would cleanse out the germs of desire. What was it that made a woman love a man with such hopeless devotion? This wretched Gavin Forbes tried to make out that whatever he did was for her benefit, yet he tossed her around sadistically. It wasn't love, Adele realised. He was reserving his more tender passion for Vivien she supposed. However ill-timed and meaningless his advances were for Adele, she knew that the taste of his charm only served to tickle her palate for more. What a fool she had been to fall for such charm. To allow herself to be exploited in the way Gavin was doing, for life at Beecroft was going to be unbearable when he visited Vivien, leaving Adele alone with suspicion. But there would be Matthew, she remembered. Dear, kind Matthew. Like Bernie in many ways, gentle in manner. The trouble was she knew she didn't love Matthew, not in a sexual way. Gavin had already accused her of stringing him along, and Matthew had suggested that his feelings for her were more than just paternal so somehow she had to make sure that Matthew knew the score.

Throughout lunch Adele avoided looking in Gavin's direction. Oliver was hungry, despite the fact that Gavin had fed him on cereal, milk, and baked beans on toast with a rasher of bacon earlier that morning, long before Adele had woken.

Perhaps Gavin had been hungry too, Adele thought, remembering the old adage that the way to a man's heart is through his stomach, for as the meal progressed the signs of strain disappeared and he was eager to tease Adele again. She found him gazing at her fondly whenever she did steal a glance. How she hated him for the speed with which his moods changed.

Lassie was reluctant to let them even talk of leaving, but Gavin in his usual adroit manner reminded his mother that Oliver had nursery school the next day, and that Vivien would want time to get used to her new habitat before going to bed.

After taking coffee round the blazing log fire in the lounge Adele excused herself to go to finish her packing. She stripped the beds and made sure that Oliver hadn't left anything in Gavin's dressing room, and when she returned to her own room she found Gavin half lying across her bed.

Her heart leapt as it always did when he looked at her in his own curious way, his greeny blue eyes full of sensuality hooded by smooth golden eyebrows.

'I'm sorry if I spoilt your weekend, Adele,' he said with a boyish grin.

She shrugged, aiming to indicate indifference.

'I suppose I spoilt yours,' she said, reminding him of the previous evening.

'Sounds as if we're playing games,' he quipped testily.

'Well, aren't we? You have two totally different moods,' she said haughtily. 'The one, the arrogant boss, the other, the devil-may-care—' she searched for a word that refused to come.

'Lover?' he taunted.

'No,' she replied quickly. 'I suppose that's the image you want to portray, but you can't quite bring yourself to . . .'

'Go on,' he urged, but she was loath to continue, her cheeks colouring deeply as words began to form which she hadn't planned to say.

'You surely don't think I'm a virgin at my age?' He got off the bed suddenly and with a laugh held Adele's shoulders roughly. 'Is that what you thought? You think I was frightened of making a fool of myself with a married woman?'

'No, such a thought never entered my head,' Adele said scornfully. 'But I do know about Anita, and I'm sorry—and I understand.'

He looked long and hard into her eyes.

'Thank you for that—lover,' he said slowly.

'Don't call me that,' she reproved hotly.

'But you are, my darling, a very irresistible lover. There's a great flood of passion waiting to be released.'

'But not for you,' she said between her teeth.

'That is what worries me, Adele.' His voice was serious, compelling as he continued: 'You're in a vulnerable state. For me that time has passed—man's needs are more basic than a woman's. You need something long-lasting—be careful that you don't give your heart away too easily.'

He turned and left her hurriedly for the second time that day.

A short while later they were all assembled in the drive-way, Gavin surrounded by cases, and hold-alls containing Vivien's belongings.

'Must you take everything in one go?' Gavin asked shortly.

'Darling, these are only my bare necessities,' Vivien insisted.

Gavin raised his eyes upward with an impatient sigh.

'Leave it to me—you all say your goodbyes and get in the car,' he ordered.

Adele motioned to Oliver, and he politely thanked Lassie for having him.

'I've loved having you, *ma chérie*,' she said, 'and your Mummy too, and I hope you'll come again soon.' She hugged and kissed Oliver then treated Adele similarly. 'I really mean that, Adele, and do think about Christmas carefully.'

Adele promised that she would and then she guided Oliver into the back seat and got in beside him. Vivien remained with Gavin trying to help, but after another blunt rejection she too said farewell to Lassie and climbed in the back seat of the luxurious Daimler.

'As soon as Jacques comes down from London I must see about getting a car again,' she explained to Adele. 'I didn't need one in London—the tube and cabs were the simplest and most efficient way of getting around up there.'

Adele looked the other way as Gavin embraced his mother. Not because she was embarrassed but because she

felt it prudent to do so, and then Gavin looked in at the
three of them, and he was smiling again.

'I see—been sent to Coventry have I?' He opened the
front passenger door and put one of the hold-alls on the
floor. 'You'll need to get yourself a hatchback or estate car
if you're always going to travel so well-loaded, Viv,' he
complained good-naturedly.

'And you need a wife, brother dear,' Viv answered back.
'You're far too bossy, and too set in your ways—but don't
expect a wife to spoil you like Lassie does.'

Gavin leaned over the front seat. 'Do you want to walk?'
he asked. 'No one can ever take Lassie's place,' he added,
and closed the door before exchanging a few more words
with his mother and getting into the driving seat. Not even
Anita? Adele wondered, as they set off through the country
lanes.

Oliver sat quietly for a few minutes then he stood up,
pushing himself against the space between the two front
seats. Adele pulled him back several times and then she
caught sight of Gavin's eyes in the mirror directed at her.

'Stop fussing, Adele. Oliver's all right—at least someone
wants to talk to me,' he said shortly.

Oliver looked round quickly at Adele to see her reaction.
She raised her eyebrows dispassionately, and then felt her
cheeks turning slightly pink as her gaze met Gavin's in the
mirror. She tried not to look again, and was thankful that
Vivien was eager to chat throughout the comparatively
short journey home. And how good it was to be home. She
had enjoyed the weekend; it was no reflection on Lassie
that she was pleased to be back at Beecroft, but Oliver too
seemed delighted to seek out his toys, and even to snuggle
happily down in his own bed after they had eaten. Gavin
and Viv had refused her offer of tea and within an hour
Gavin had called goodbye and left.

Vivien settled in quickly, not that Adele saw much of her
except occasionally in the evenings and then one afternoon
just after lunch when Oliver was having a nap, the doorbell
rang. Adele opened it and the surprise must have shown in

her face. It was like looking at Gavin's twin.

'Hello,' he said, with a flashing smile, 'You, I think, will be the lovely Adele—please—allow me to introduce myself—Jacques.' He held out a smooth be-ringed hand.

'How do you do,' Adele answered flattered by his compliment, dazzled by his good looks and sexy French accent. 'I expect you want Vivien,' she added.

Huge dark eyes—the only difference between him and his cousin Gavin, Adele thought—surveyed her intimately saying so much more than words would have done.

'I have come to see Vivien,' he said in a low suggestive voice.

'There's a door by the garage,' Adele recited automatically, still mesmerised by the effluent charm of the Frenchman. 'There's a bell—it has Viv's name on it,' she explained.

'I know—I saw it—I also saw a large Volvo in the garage—the door remains open, you see.'

He stood back and pointed to Bernie's car.

'That's my husband's,' Adele said, then added quickly: 'was my husband's—he died over six months ago.'

'I know that too—and I offer you my humblest condolences.' A serious mask came down over his face, and his expression was one of compassion. 'I realise that I may be speaking out of turn, Madame, but, I wondered—what you intend to do with this car?'

Adele shrugged, a cold misery creeping over her briefly as she was reminded yet again that this was one decision she simply must make soon. She sighed deeply. 'I suppose I'll have to sell it eventually,' she said. 'It's too large for Oliver and me—I'm happy with my own smaller car.'

'Women are too delicate to have to deal with such things, Madame,' he said kindly, 'but surely you must know that it can only deteriorate standing here?'

Adele nodded. 'So Matthew keeps reminding me. I must ask the garage about it when I go in next time.'

'Adele,' Jacques spoke softly, returning to the open doorway and taking the privilege of stepping inside. 'I know it must pain you to do this—perhaps you would prefer to sell it to the garage who can see that it goes to another town, or perhaps you would like to feel that a friend is looking after it—someone who has a passion for cars, Adele—and would cherish it as he would a woman—like me, for instance?'

Now that she was getting used to this man she could see that he was much darker than Gavin, yet there were hints of burnished gold in his hair and also in the thin moustache, and even though his eyes were a different colour from Gavin's it was the charm, the smile, some hidden yet distinguishable quality which marked and characterised the two men as being so alike.

'I . . . I'll have to think about it,' she said with a nervous laugh. 'I know it would be sensible . . . but, I'll let you know.'

'I am here for just one week longer to see our agency in action then I shall need a car for travelling to and from London.'

'I promise I'll try to make up my mind by then,' she said, and he moved away to Vivien's front door.

Adele felt quite breathless, but she knew that it was a decision she couldn't put off any longer. To let Jacques have Bernie's Volvo would save her a lot of unnecessary discussion with the garage, although she knew that she had only to mention it to Matthew and he would have attended to it for her. But things had changed since her weekend in the country. Matthew still called, but Adele discovered, more frequently to visit Vivien. At first she had thought his interest purely professional, but it had come as a shock on one occasion to see his car disappearing out of the driveway one night at close on midnight. Oliver had cried out in his sleep and she had got up to go to him, then hearing a noise she had looked out of her bedroom window to see Matthew driving away down the road. She had lain in bed suddenly wide awake to what was happening. A slight pang perhaps at rejection, but short-lived as she realised how entirely suited Matthew and Vivien were. But did Gavin know? Was he to be hurt yet again? She constantly relived the precious intimate moments they had shared at Cedar

Grove. She knew that she had made a terrible mistake in declaring her love for him because that had changed everything. It proved conclusively, of course, that he didn't love her. She despised herself for her provocative behaviour, realising now that all he wanted was a little fun, and she had taken it all too seriously.

His words to her now were few. A polite 'Good morning' each morning except on Mondays, when he would say: 'Good morning, Adele—everything all right?' It didn't even give her room to hold a conversation with him and now she didn't look surreptitiously at him with adulation because she couldn't bear to. Above all she had to try to show him that it had all been a mad impulsive moment and that she really didn't care. It wasn't easy to disguise her emotions because she did care very much, and there were times when she felt angry, and hurt for Oliver.

Gavin was clever. He didn't neglect Oliver altogether. He would leave a message for Adele with Sheila or the receptionist, telling her to take Oliver into the clinic while she was at the club for a session in the gym and a sauna, and two hours later she would pick Oliver up at the club and hear how Uncle Gavin had taken him to the park to feed the ducks, or to the swing-park.

She desperately wished that everything could be the same as it had been in the beginning, but in his way Gavin was telling her that any romance she had read into it was over. She was grateful for Matthew's continued loyalty. She knew that on Sunday evenings when he visited her after golf and some time spent socially at his club that he would sit sipping his drink silently observing her. Occasionally some point of interest would arise concerning *A Votre Santé* clinic, but Adele did her best to avoid any mention of Gavin and his interests, as well as the fact that she knew Matthew frequently called on Vivien.

'I hear Viv's going to baby-sit for you to go to the Christmas party at the clinic,' he said suddenly one evening.

'She has offered, but I feel she should be the one to be going. I'm not really into parties. I know I must make an effort at Christmas for Oliver's sake but—well—you know,' she finished lamely with a shrug.

'Viv feels equally adamant about it being you who goes to the party. Besides Gavin will insist upon it, but I'll come and escort you if you'd like me to.'

'Thanks, I'd like that—if I can't find a way of getting out of going,' Adele said.

Matthew smiled endearingly. 'No way,' he assured her. 'After that the clinic closes down for the week prior to Christmas—it's always quiet, and as everyone has so much to do it's better to shut down completely. Have you seen your dress yet?'

'My dress?'

'Our Gavin thinks of everything, my dear,' Matthew said with a sly grin. 'He hates name tabs at a social function so he thinks if his staff wear similar dresses you're instantly recognisable.'

'I thought it was a party,' Adele said laughing.

'It is—and a good one—and don't under-estimate your boss. Viv and Jacques—well, more Jacques I believe, have designed your dresses. Green and white, naturally, being the clinic colours. Jacques will be bringing them back from London next weekend. By the way, my dear, I think that was most sensible of you to let Jacques have the car.'

'It's only a car, after all,' Adele said. 'I missed seeing it at first, but now that Viv has hers it doesn't seem so bad.'

'You're quite happy with Viv here?—everything is working out all right between you?' Matthew asked, and Adele knew what he wanted to hear.

'We get along very well, she's a super person, and I'm very happy for you, Matthew.' Adele poked him in the ribs jovially. Matthew gathered her in his arms and hugged her.

'You did turn me down, Adele,' he reminded her, 'and I was jealous of Gavin at one point—but it was love at first sight for Viv and me.'

'Then I'm really pleased—you are ideally suited I'd say.'

'I'd like to see you happy too, my dear,' Matthew said.

'Now don't let's be morbid—it is nearly Christmas, after all—I'm young, so everyone keeps telling me, so there's plenty of time— besides, I have Oliver.'

'And he needs a father.'

'Hundreds of women have brought up children quite successfully on their own—I can do the same,' she stated emphatically.

Matthew walked round the room thoughtfully.

'I hear you're coming to Cedar Grove too for Christmas?'

'We were invited, but I said no because it's better for Oliver to remain in his own home.'

'Adele—I shall go because I want to be with Viv. You're going to hate it here—it'll be so quiet.'

'Don't worry about us, Matthew. You've been a tower of strength, and I can never repay you for all your kindness and the love and care you've given to Oliver and me, but now I'm coming to terms with life again. Oliver has made friends with several children at nursery school, so naturally I've made friends with some of the Mums. We've had lots of invitations, really,' she said, a little too brightly, 'but in the end I expect we shall fly off to Canada. Every week Mum and Dad ring to try to persuade me.'

'Well you'll have to make haste and book, my dear, or you'll never get a plane.'

'Yes, I know, I must deal with it,' but she knew in her heart that she didn't want to go to Canada—that was just a little too far away from Gavin . . .

Adele threw herself into preparations for Christmas. She purchased a tree and Oliver helped her to decorate it. She posted the usual cards and spent hours shopping for Oliver—and deep inside her the pain intensified. Matthew had been right, of course, Christmas at Beecroft with just the two of them was going to be unbearable. Fortunately there was plenty going on at the nursery school for Oliver, and one afternoon she went to the little show they put on, and at Sunday School Oliver was one of the Three Wise Men in a nativity play, but Adele could only look on through a veil of tears and try to hide the ache in her heart. People had been so kind to her, helping her over the hurdles of life immediately after Bernie's death, but now Christmas was the biggest hurdle of all.

The clinic was busy with an ever increasing demand for clients to be medically screened, and with the usual problems of an English climate once one member of the staff went down with flu it hit the remainder, all except Adele. She had the hint of a cold but after a visit to the sauna it mysteriously disappeared and so it fell to her to work longer hours.

Oliver was quite happy now to go with other people, sometimes Jonathan's mother would pick him up from nursery school and on other occasions Mrs Dawkins took him home with her until Adele had finished. In a way it was a respite for Adele from too much time to brood. A hectic ten days, working during the mornings and afternoons, and making preparations for Christmas in the evenings after Oliver had gone to bed. It was a comfort to know that Vivien was in the house, often Matthew as well but she yearned to open the door, or pick up the telephone and find Gavin wanting to see her, but after a particularly bad bout of flu he still remained aloof and she watched him seemingly to grow older and look more depressed. Then as Matthew and Vivien's relationship continued, Adele realised that he must be suffering from a bad case of having been jilted. Of course this was the obvious reason which prevented him from coming to Beecroft any more. This knowledge only served to distress Adele. She wanted to comfort him, but that wouldn't help Gavin if he loved Vivien. Life was so complicated. It hadn't been for her and Bernie, she recalled, there had been no side involvements, no one else to cause petty jealousies, they had met, fallen in love and been loyal to each other. If nothing else, she thought, as she sprayed some leaves with silver dust, I've got my memories. But memories are in the mind, and she was made of flesh and blood. She knew that Gavin had aroused all the instincts of human life so how could she survive a lifetime on memories? Perhaps Canada was the best solution after all, not just for Christmas, but for good. Away from everything perhaps the memories would fade more quickly, but again, the thought of Gavin, occasionally seeing and talking to him, the knowledge that he was never too far away forced immigration out of her mind.

Tucked away in a small attic room she had been unaware of any activity in the house but suddenly she heard her name being called and she opened the door. Halfway down the short flight of stairs she saw Vivien.

'Whatever are you doing up there?' Viv asked.

'Ssh—Christmas, and all that—what's wrong, did Oliver call?'

'No—come on down to try on your dress for Gavin's party.'

Adele looked at her sticky hands. 'I'm not fit to be near anything good—can you give me half an hour?'

'Sure—come on in my place when you're ready.'

Adele was thankful that for once Matthew was not visiting and she gasped with pleasure when she walked into Vivien's lounge.

'You have to admit, Adele, that Gavin has an eye for colour—it is a gorgeous shade of green, he chose this material because of the water wave in it, and with the white bodice—what there is of it—'

'It's a bit revealing for me,' Adele said slipping off her housecoat.

'You're losing weight again, my girl, and in this dress the boss will notice, and he has a thing about skinny women.'

'Thank you,' Adele laughed.

'You've still got a good figure though, and a long dress is always so elegant.'

Vivien zipped her up and re-arranged the white nylon rose on the shoulder then stood back to survey Adele in her finery.

'Mm—you look stunning, Adele—that colour really suits you—mm—I did wonder if I might have to pad the bust, but it fits rather well—lucky you.'

Adele eyed herself in the mirror with some misgivings—it really was rather low cut for her, but to be wearing an evening dress again—her boss's hostess—she hoped she could perform her function as Gavin would expect. She wanted to because she loved him—each day made her more aware of that, even though his attitude towards her remained polite but cool. He had enjoyed his moments of sensual pleasure with her. Showing her that she was not as emotionally dead as she had believed, but when she had allowed herself to become extrovert in his company he evidently thought they had gone far enough. He had insinuated on numerous occasions that Matthew wanted her, how galling it must be for him now to find that Matthew had won Viv away from him.

On the morning of the party while Adele was decorating the lounges to be used that evening Matthew emerged from Gavin's office, leaving the door ajar.

'Adele, my dear,' he said, his voice full of concern, 'I'm not as free today as I had hoped. An important case scheduled for theatre this afternoon. You know how these things are, it may last several hours. I'm sorry to have to let you down, Adele, but I'm not at all sure that I can pick you up this evening. It might be better to make other arrangements.'

'I can drive myself,' Adele volunteered readily. 'I'd rather, honestly, Matthew. I can be quite independent, you see, although,' she added a hint mischievously, 'I'd give anything for a sudden bout of flu.'

'Now you know you don't mean that,' he laughed, his hand automatically sliding round her waist as he indulged in a gentle squeeze. 'You'll have a good time, you'll see, and save a dance for me, I shall get here eventually.'

'Dancing? Here? I hadn't realised,' Adele said, echoing some disappointment. 'I thought it was a cocktail party, a sort of publicity function.'

'It's all of those things—now you just make up your mind to enjoy yourself, my dear. Are you sure you wouldn't rather take a taxi in so that I can drive you home—or I could ask Gavin.'

'No,' Adele answered sharply. 'Really, Matthew, I'll manage,' she assured him.

Gavin strode out of his office at that moment bent on reclaiming Matthew's attention over some business matter. He glanced absent-mindedly in Adele's direction, but she accepted this with a measure of hurt, realising how he despised her. He had not even bothered to confirm that Oliver was to be taken care of while she was at the party. It would serve him right, she thought, if she chose not to turn up. But Vivien would have related the details of their arrangements. They must communicate at some time if only by telephone, and now Adele knew that she wanted to go to the party. Matthew had mentioned dancing. Was there a glimmer of hope that she might find herself in Gavin's arms, and that in such close contact she could draw him back to her into the same relationship they had enjoyed at Cedar Grove? Was she clever enough to woo him out of his frustration at losing Vivien to Matthew? She would be discreet, but it was worth a try. If only there was some way of making him realise that she had been honest in the declaration of her love for him. She hadn't wanted it to happen. Hadn't she tried to resist against any involvement? It was still early days. She had a lifetime in which to develop her social life, meet new people, find herself again. Was she mistaking infatuation for his flattery and attentions for love? Whatever it was, which ever path she chose to tread there seemed only misery and pain, so she might as well grasp any opportunity which came along to enjoy herself.

As soon as she and Oliver had finished their lunch Oliver went to bed as usual, and Adele went outside to clear out her car. Almost immediately she heard the purr of a familiar car engine and looked down the drive to see the Volvo turning in. She didn't know why the arrival of Gavin's cousin should cause her heart to miss a beat and her cheeks to flush in embarrassment. Was it because of his close relationship with the man she loved? Or was she still stirred at the sight of Bernie's car?

Jacques strolled towards her casually.

'Adele,' he greeted, holding out his hand formally.

Could he feel hers trembling? she wondered, and then reproached herself for such stupidity.

'I'd like to think that the blush was for me,' Jacques said softly.

'I . . . I'm going out as soon as Oliver wakes,' she

informed him.

'I'm glad that I caught you then—I wondered if you have an escort for the party this evening?'

'Well—Matthew would have taken me, but he's rather tied up at the hospital. I can easily drive myself though.'

'Please—allow me—I would so much like to, Adele.'

'But I won't be there to enjoy myself, Jacques, I'm a hostess, I understand—whatever that may mean.'

'I can tell you that, *ma chérie*. You are there to look lovely, to be lovely, and to be seen to be charming to the gentlemen present, and I hope that will include me. Now you really can't drive yourself in a long gown, which Vivien tells me suits you—your—' he outlined her figure with his hands—'you admirably.' His dark eyes glided down the length of her tight-fitting jeans, and up to challenge the recognition in her own equally dark-brown eyes.

'Well, I can take a taxi then,' she suggested.

'No—I will be honoured to escort you. Now, I must have a word with Vivien—until seven o'clock—' he gave her a knowing wink and Adele rushed into the house and stood with her back against the door. Whew! What did you say to discourage a persistent Frenchman? She didn't want to go with anyone—no-one but Gavin, of course, and he hadn' even offered.

She was glad when Oliver woke and grateful too that Jonathan's mother had agreed to have Oliver for an hour while she had a sauna. The sauna was the one place where she found she could totally relax. It did her skin good was her excuse, but she knew that it restored her both physically and mentally.

She sat back in the sauna watching the beads of perspiration trickle down her skin. Whenever she came she remembered the time she had stayed too long. There was no fear of her doing that now, or of it affecting her in any way as she had become thoroughly accustomed to the heat. She shampooed her hair under the shower at the club recalling the excitement of standing with Gavin under the soft spraying water at Cedar Grove. She felt quite certain that Lassie would not have approved, unless it had been Viv there with

him. Poor Lassie, what unhappiness was she suffering now
that Viv and Matthew had become so close?

With thoughts of Gavin, and the need to look her very
best for him tonight, she spent fifteen minutes on the
sun-bed in the club's solarium hoping that the regular
treatment was preserving the light tan she had acquired
during the summer. She supposed Gavin wouldn't even
notice, but she intended to make an all out effort to be as
provocative as protocol allowed.

She realised she had been at the club a fair time, so
flushed and radiant she hurried towards the exit and half-
way down the wrought-iron spiral staircase she collided
with a figure on his way up.

Gavin made no move to allow her to pass.

'Making yourself beautiful for tonight?' he questioned
lightly.

Why did he have to use a tone which made it sound as if
making herself beautiful was promiscuous?

'I come regularly,' she retorted shortly.

'I do remember,' he replied in a low voice causing her
already pink cheeks to turn a deeper colour. 'I'm glad you
don't make a habit of overdoing things.'

'One experience like that was enough,' she said quickly,
and one of his elegant straw-coloured eyebrows shot up to
accompany a surreptitious smile.

'I shall have to be back this evening early,' he said. 'I'll
pick you up at around—six-thirty?' He managed to raise his
voice on the time turning it into a question, but as usual he
was taking everything for granted.

'I have a lift in, thank you,' she said.

'But Matthew—' he began.

'No, I know Matthew can't bring me,' she interrupted
hastily. 'I've had another offer.'

Both eyebrows were raised albeit briefly before the mask
of disapproval covered his face.

'Good, then I'll see you and your partner here, fair
damsel, but I shall expect you to circulate, of course.'

He stood aside to let her pass and she ran all the way
along the subway to the car park, her cheeks blazing.

CHAPTER TEN

DAMN and blast Jacques, she thought aggressively fumbling
with the lock on the car door. Why had she allowed him to
persuade her so easily before she had given Gavin time to
offer his services? But he had known about Matthew's
appointment this morning. Had he deliberately postponed
his offer knowing that by now she would have made
alternative arrangements? Did he know it was Jacques?
No, by the reference to 'her partner' he probably didn't,
but by this evening he would if the two men were as close as
she imagined they would be, especially as Jacques would
almost certainly be staying at Gavin's flat.

She managed to calm herself and by the time she picked
Oliver up she was bordering on high spirits just as she had
been in anticipation of hospital dances some years before.

Oliver had had tea with Jonathan so Adele bathed and
prepared him for bed then sat on the edge of his bed while
she painted a pearly pink varnish on finger and toe-nails.
While they dried she read a story and Oliver thought it
great fun to hold the book and turn the pages for her.

He was no problem to leave, that was a comfort to her,
and he was almost as besotted with Vivien as he was with
Gavin.

Vivien came down in good time helping Adele to put the
finishing touches to her appearance.

'You know,' Viv said, taking stock, 'we could use you in
the agency—it's a glam job, and if you could stay slim, and
with a few lessons in deportment you'd be good.'

'I'm the mother of a four year old,' Adele said laughing.

'And you're going to be swept off your feet one of these
days, and then watch the pounds return with sheer content-
ment,' Viv predicted. 'There—you do look quite something.'

'So I should,' Adele quipped, 'with the experts to help me.'

She paraded before the long mirror. The dress was a shimmering vision of elegance, the long slim-line sleeves, one white, one green in accordance with the two-coloured bodice added length to her already adequate height, as did the long white insert to one side of the skirt, narrow at the waist, widening as it reached the floor. The neckline was low and wide, shaped to reveal a bare cleavage. A green nylon rose was attached to the waist at the narrow end of the long white insertion in the skirt. At first she had decided against jewellery, but Vivien had persuaded her to wear a simple short gold chain round her neck with small stud ear-rings to match, and her gold court evening shoes were very high-heeled.

Vivien pushed her gold clutch bag into her hand.

'There—complete—you'll have to be careful your fur cape doesn't crush the roses. Gavin will be proud of you.'

'He won't even notice if we're all dressed the same,' Adele said with a smirk.

'I wouldn't bank on that,' Viv told her and a long impatient ring on the doorbell sent Viv downstairs to let Jacques in.

'I've brought him up to say goodnight to Oliver,' Viv said, as they all assembled in his bedroom.

Oliver's large dark eyes appraised Adele with a warmth and admiration she wouldn't have expected to see in a four year old.

'Just like the queen, Mummy,' he said, his face radiant.

'Be a good boy, darling,' Adele whispered and kissed him gently before leaving him. She always felt a stirring of emotion when she left him in other people's care and it showed in her eyes.

'He'll be fine with me, Adele,' Viv assured her. 'There's no more school, no more clinic, so he doesn't have to settle down for another half hour. I'm going to enjoy having him all to myself.'

'You should be the one to be going to the party,' Adele said.

'I've still got to take care, according to Matthew. Give me six months and I'll enjoy getting back into the social whirl again. You go off and *have fun!*' she ordered.

'How can so charming a woman not have fun?' Jacques said, and as they reached the hall he turned, and Adele was impressed at his immaculate appearance. Not that he wasn't always well-dressed, but sometimes a little too stylistic for her tastes. Now in evening dress he looked more handsome than ever, and so much like Gavin in features. Her spirits lifted immediately at the thought of her beloved. Tonight he would have to notice her, she would make sure that he did.

Adele could hardly contain her gasp of admiration when they did come face to face. Jacques was a pleasant person to be with and had appreciated her emotional feelings at sitting beside him in what had been Bernie's Volvo, so he had been boyishly light-hearted making her laugh during the short journey to the clinic, and they were both exchanging mischievous banter as they reached the reception area.

'Ah, Gavin,' Jacques greeted his cousin, 'I have much pleasure in bringing you one of your delightful ladies, but I hope you will not make her work too hard, or keep her all to yourself.'

Gavin's eyes were intense, and the most iridescent green she had ever noticed before. He appeared not to be amused.

'Enjoying yourself is not usually considered hard work,' he replied coolly. 'I don't think Adele will find it unpleasant to circulate.' He almost nodded dismissal as Sheila came up to him and linked her arm through his. Of course, Adele thought miserably, the boss and his head nurse. Thank goodness she had Jacques who was sophisticated and attentive. A little too smooth perhaps—oh hell, she thought angrily, Jacques doesn't even compare with Gavin.

The night was young, the first of the guests just arriving, Sheila couldn't stay glued to Gavin throughout the evening.

The waiting staff of the catering firm Gavin had hired brought a tray of sherry and Adele took one, sipping it thirstily to gain moral courage.

Almost as if Gavin intended to separate her and Jacques he introduced some early guests, suggesting that they go through to the spacious lounge where a piano had been brought in and a male pianist filled the atmosphere with soft melody.

As more clients arrived her guests moved on to circulate and she was never allowed to stand for more than a minute before Gavin would introduce her to someone else. Laughter and chatter echoed, sometimes drowning the romantic music but everyone seemed to be enjoying themselves and Adele had to put on a cloak of conviviality.

Jacques never got back to her but was soon seeking out the delights of other female company, and when Adele noticed Gavin and Sheila come through to the lounge with some guests she edged her way round to the open doors and slipped back to the reception area.

She arrived just as Matthew did.

'Adele—my dear—you look enchanting,' he praised.

She tucked her arm through his companionably.

'Can I hostess you, Matthew?—I've run out of small talk.'

Matthew stooped to kiss her. 'You won't need small talk when the eats have all gone and the lights go down—that's when the smooching and the dancing start.'

'Oh dear,' Adele groaned. 'Not one of those parties.'

'Not intentionally, but human nature being what it is—you put a few glamorous women into a room and whoopee!'

'You sound quite frivolous—for you,' Adele laughed up at him.

'Thank you. There's life in the old dog yet you know.' He bent low and whispered in her ear. 'I've just come from Beecroft.'

'You cheat!' Adele said. 'No wonder I was delegated to Jacques.'

'I was kept late at the hospital, my dear, but I couldn't resist the temptation to pop in and see Viv—and Oliver, of course. She was teaching him to play draughts—he's having a high old time.'

'You really are in love, Matthew—for the very first time?'

Matthew looked into Adele's face fondly. 'Mm—not quite—there was once this pretty blonde nurse with rich, velvety brown eyes—I did what I could for her when she was left a sad and young—much too young widow—but she fell in love with someone else.'

'Stop it, Matthew—it wasn't like that at all—you're the one who fell in love—and I do believe it was for the very first time—you're crazily in love with Viv, and she with you. Poor Gavin—no wonder he's so sour.'

'Gavin? Sour? I hadn't noticed. He does have a serious side to his nature—but he believes that's necessary to run a business efficiently. But Gavin and Viv? Whatever gave you that idea?'

'They are only step-brother and sister, Matthew, and until you claimed Viv I think they were—well—involved?'

Matthew disengaged her hand from his arm as he took a drink from a passing waiter, then as he sipped he looked down into her eyes. 'As far as I know, my dear, there has never been anything between them—Gavin is free—so it's entirely up to you.'

Adele felt her cheeks flushing a deeper roseate hue.

'Does it really show?' she asked shyly.

'It has for a very long time, my dear. When you went to Cedar Grove I thought everything would sort itself out.'

'It did in *my* mind,' Adele said softly with a despondent sigh. 'That's the trouble, I took him and everything he did all too seriously. When he's nice he's only being kind out of sympathy, and mainly for Oliver's sake. Did you know that he was nearly married—but she died?'

Matthew nodded. 'Of course—that's why he seemed a suitable employer for you—he of all people understood how you were feeling.'

'I don't recall that he showed me any special favours, or was even very pleasant on my first day,' she said.

'That's Gavin's manner—the show must go on kind of attitude—and it worked, Adele—it worked wonders—it shook you out of that inertia to carry on merely for Oliver's sake. You started to live again yourself.'

'And look where that got me,' she replied dismally.

'You can't have everything at once, my dear, but you are much happier than you were.'

'There were moments—magic ones, when I thought Gavin felt the same way, but,' she shrugged, trying to make light of it, 'he doesn't, so that's it. Now you know why I couldn't bear to go to Cedar Grove for Christmas. The agony of loving him and knowing that he doesn't love me.' Her voice trembled with emotion. 'Please, Matthew, that's in confidence,' she added earnestly, realising that she had opened her heart to him in a much more intimate way than she had intended.

'There's still plenty of time, my dear,' Matthew whispered and together they mingled with the guests as the refreshments were served.

Matthew seemed contented to keep her as his companion as they circulated among colleagues, and later when the lights were lowered and the pianist echoed a more romantic mood Matthew took Adele in his arms to dance. They were gliding past a huge wall mirror and in it Adele's eyes became hypnotised by a pair of piercing green ones surveying her and Matthew with a look of extreme distaste.

She couldn't imagine what she had done to irritate him, except of course to have told him that she loved him. Did he despise her so much? Perhaps a few moments in his embrace, even the most casual of dances would help to break down the barrier which had sprung up between them. Oh, how she longed to dance with him, but it was Jacques who interrupted the liaison between her and Matthew, and Jacques who managed with his persuasive charm to make her smile again.

The party continued until midnight and by then some guests were leaving. Gavin was at the door looking reasonably satisfied as he said goodnight to everyone as well as wishing them a happy Christmas.

Adele prepared to leave too, and was looking round for Matthew when Jacques returned to her side.

'I brought you, Madame, so I think I can claim a right to

taking you home,' he said with a disarming smile.

Adele was at a loss for words. She had assumed Matthew would have driven her home and as if her dilemma had been broadcast suddenly Gavin and Matthew attached themselves to her and Jacques.

'I shall have to be the last person to leave, Adele, so I can't expect you to wait for me,' Gavin said abruptly—as if she had intended to anyway, she thought, as she turned hopefully towards Matthew, but Jacques was in command.

'I had the honour to escort the charming lady so it is my duty to see her safely home,' he said.

Matthew smiled down at her reassuringly and she couldn't bear to look at Gavin for surely he would recognise the disappointment in her eyes.

'Thank you for being a delightful hostess for me, fair damsel,' Gavin said, holding out his hand. She raised her eyes hesitantly as she placed her hand in his, and the warmth from him sent a glow of exhilaration through her body. 'I hope you've enjoyed yourself at the same time.' He smiled, but she regarded it as a false sentiment and her heart sank again. His green eyes were cold, ice-cold, surveying her with a look of silent reproach. She managed to mumble goodnight and tossed the same to Matthew over her shoulder sensing that the two men were anxious to hold a conversation. She sat beside Jacques in the Volvo, tense and uncommunicative, desperately trusting that Matthew would honour her confidence.

The weather had turned extremely cold and there were patches of ice on the road so that she was pleased when Jacques pulled into the drive.

She looked across at him. 'It's been a lovely evening and thank you for being my escort,' she said. He answered by merely taking her chin between his fingers, fingers that were surprisingly warm, then he opened the door, got out and went round to her side.

'Got your key handy?' he asked in a hushed whisper. The house was silent and in darkness. She found her key by the interior light of the car and he helped her out, taking the key from her and unlocking the door.

To her surprise he followed her in, closing the door behind him gently, and taking off his coat. She went into the lounge and he was beside her in a moment helping her off with her fur cape.

'I must just see Oliver,' she said and skipped away out of his reach, and as she stood peering down at the flushed face and ruffled mop of black curls she wondered how she was going to tactfully dismiss Jacques.

When she returned to the lounge he wasn't there so she followed the muted sounds which came from the kitchen.

'He is all right?' Jacques asked casually turning from the stove.

'Fast asleep,' Adele replied, noticing that two mugs had been removed from the mug-tree, and milk was already warming in a saucepan on the stove.

Just like his cousin, she thought, domineering, arrogant, and always in charge. She surveyed the back of him, a trifle leaner than Gavin, but still with the same elegance of masculine virility oozing even from the cut of his dinner jacket.

'After so much wine, coffee would be nice I thought—you see—how domesticated I am?'

Adele laughed meekly. 'Did you want anything to eat?' she asked.

Jacques appeared to be considering this as he poured the hot milk into the mugs on top of the instant coffee.

'I think not—poor coffee, I am afraid, but quick.'

Adele found a small tray and Jacques carried them through to the lounge where Adele switched on the gas fire.

'The heating is on a low setting—perhaps I ought to put it up if it's going to freeze,' she said absent-mindedly.

'You will need to keep it on permanently if the snow comes as forecast,' Jacques suggested. 'This will be your first winter alone, Adele, but your last I feel sure. It isn't right that a woman should have to cope alone with a house this size—and your boy needs a father.'

'We shall manage,' she answered quietly.

'Of course—because you must—but you must impel your life, Adele, nothing stands still.'

She sipped her coffee slowly, coffee which she hadn't really wanted.

'When are you going to Cedar Grove?' he asked suddenly.

'We're not—we're staying here,' she explained. 'Children are always best in their own home at Christmas time.'

'Alone? Just the two of you?—*ma chérie—Non!* This must not be—Christmas is a time of festivity—a time of fun for children—Adele—you must come to Paris with me.'

Adele stared at him open-mouthed, then she laughed as light-heartedly as she could.

'We shall be fine—I *want* to stay here,' she said adamantly.

'You shall come to my family—I 'ave two sisters, married with children—Oliver would have a splendid time—and we—my sweet Adele, will have time to get to know one another—time to learn to love—'

Suddenly she was in his arms, crushed against the white frill of his shirt, and his lips closed over hers with such violence that she swayed against him in apparent surrender.

They had been sitting at opposite ends of the settee, now he pushed her head back on the cushion resting on the arm, and he lay over the length of her his kisses so paralysing that she struggled in vain. She closed her eyes, an inane plea to Gavin forced from her lips as she fought against the wiles of the passionate Frenchman.

His experienced fingers seemed to explore her all over, and with disgust she realised that he had craftily slid down her zip so that the beautiful green and white dress lay crumpled between them, her breasts and waist bare which, as she heaved against Jacques only provoked him the more. She twisted her head from side to side in an effort to speak, but he found this delightfully inviting, and his kisses and impetuous love-making was more frenzied than anything she had ever known so that she became consumed with a desperate anger, and on a furious impulse she dragged her painted fingernails down his cheeks.

For a horrified moment Adele thought that he didn't

register any pain, but slowly he raised his head from her bosom and she saw that his cheeks were scored with bright red weals.

'Let me get up,' she demanded hotly, her eyes blazing hatred, her cheeks flushed with rage.

'*Ma chérie,*' he whispered seductively. 'You are a woman—you have feelings—you are warm and so beautiful.'

Somehow she managed to wriggle out from under him, at the same time pushing against him so that he was obliged to stand up.

'How dare you take such a liberty in my house,' she accused. 'Oliver upstairs asleep—Vivien in the house.'

He splayed his hands in a nonchalant gesture.

'So? They cannot see through the walls and ceilings. You are too modest, my sweet Adele—come let us undress before the fire and make love—yes?'

'No! You blasted men are all the same—you think because I have been left a widow that I'm desperate for sex—well I'm *not*! I'm old-fashioned, Jacques, and I believe in love.'

'We make love first—you learn to love each other a little more each time—there is no passion on earth like a Frenchman's—see, I care for your body, Adele.' He took a step nearer.

'There's no deeper love and understanding than an Englishman's, Jacques—and that is what *I* crave for.'

'You are in love with an Englishman?'

'Yes—but the fact that he doesn't love me makes no difference—I'm not free to any man who wants to satisfy his lust.'

'You are being hard on me, Adele—you spit like a cat, and your claws are equally sharp.' He put a finger up to his cheek and wiped away a drop of blood. 'This man you love—he had better soon take you—or I shall have pleasure in doing so—I could do so now—no woman gets the better of me, Adele, in fact, ravishment holds a certain enticement.'

'Don't force me to call the police, Jacques. You've

evidently had too much to drink—or I could call Gavin.'

Jacques eyed her with suspicion.

'Gavin? What is he to you? Ah—I see now—you wish to save yourself for him—of course, you have both suffered similarly.' He nodded, a look of understanding reflected in his expression. 'So, you think you love Gavin?'

'I don't think, I know,' she said firmly, 'but he doesn't love me.'

'Then the man's a fool.' He continued to stare at her. 'You flirt a little, with me, with Matthew, in order to make my cousin jealous, is that it?'

'Now you're being ridiculous. I haven't flirted with anyone—Matthew is an old and much valued friend. Will you please go, Jacques? I want to go to bed.'

He sighed. 'To bed—such an invitation, Adele—but it would not be good for your son to wake in the morning and find a man beside his *maman*.'

Adele's patience snapped at his audacity. 'Get out!' she shrieked.

'Yes, I will do that, Adele—and while you are spending Christmas alone here remember the ecstasy you could have known—tonight, and in Paris. I shall return after Christmas—beware, *ma chérie*—I shall not give up easily.' He swaggered across the room, took his car coat from the rack and went out, stumbling a little on the threshold. Adele helped him on his way by pushing the door, locking it and securing the chain.

She had gathered the dress up round the front of her, now she let it fall to the ground, and returning to the lounge she draped it over the arm of one of the chairs. Left only in briefs and tights she turned everything off and ran upstairs to her bedroom. Before she switched on a light she peeped out between the curtains in time to see the Volvo backing out of the drive. Was Jacques going back to Gavin's flat? How was he going to explain the scratches on his cheeks? But that didn't matter to Adele—she simply didn't care. She fell asleep almost as soon as her head touched the pillow, and in the morning she got up eagerly having made an important decision.

She was still young, reasonably attractive, she supposed, and with a nice house of her own and financial security she realised that she was easy prey for the opposite sex. It would do her good to get away for a while—she hated the thought of being far away from Gavin—but she felt the need of the comfort and love her parents were anxious to give her. But when Oliver greeted her cheerfully she guessed that he would be happiest at home. He had been invited to one or two parties so for this reason Adele put off her visit to the travel agency, and when she did go she discovered that all the seats to Canada were already booked, the only hope was for her to go to the airport on standby.

Her decision had not been such a sensible one after all, but when she got home Matthew's car was in the drive and as Adele was unlocking her front door Vivien came down from her flat.

'Adele—can I come in for a minute?'

'Of course—shall I make some tea? Oliver's at a party.'

'Well, I'd rather not stop—unless—will you come to Cedar Grove, Adele?' Vivien pleaded. 'If you will we'll wait until you've fetched Oliver, but the snow is on its way so we wanted to get going before we're all housebound. We'd stay here with you, but then it means Lassie and Gavin will spend Christmas on their own.'

Adele hesitated. The offer was tempting, but what did Gavin want? He hadn't telephoned or visited, and the last thing she wanted was to embarrass him by changing her mind.

'I'm afraid this is the last chance, Adele, unless you can find your own way up there, as Gavin is already there,' Vivien explained.

Adele experienced a tightening up of all her muscles. So he didn't want her to go and he'd gone early to indicate that he didn't.

'It's very kind of you, Viv,' Adele said quietly, 'But no, we're going to stay and make sure the house keeps warm and free from freeze-ups. Have a good time, and give my love to Lassie.'

'We're disappointed, Adele—Lassie was so hoping you'd come, but she understands and didn't want to bring too much pressure to bear—as she said, the decision has to be yours. By the way, forgive my mentioning it but Jacques is safely in Paris—he won't bother you over Christmas.'

Adele looked questioningly at Vivien, who smiled and went on: 'You handled him well, Adele. He's a tyrant after a couple of drinks.' She laughed. 'At any time really.'

'You evidently heard?'

'I heard noises, and usually you're so quiet, so I looked out and saw the Volvo. I was all ready to come to your assistance—most of all in case Oliver woke, but you should be congratulated on your successful handling in a difficult situation.'

'I didn't know I could handle such a situation. I'm beginning to realise how many and varied are the types of men—I just hope I can steer clear of them in future.'

'You need the right one to protect you, Adele,' Vivien said. 'Well, if you're sure about not coming to Cedar Grove we'll be off. I hate doing it—and I'm sure they're empty words if I wish you a happy Christmas—but we'll telephone you and Oliver on Christmas morning.'

And I won't be here, I hope, Adele thought, confused and disappointed by Gavin's lack of friendship, but the decision now to go to Canada seemed the right one, as she explained to Oliver when she drove him home from the party.

'We might even have to sleep at the airport,' she said, hoping the adventure might be an inducement to her young son.

'But I don't want to go to Canada, Mummy,' he wailed. 'I wanted to see Honey and Uncle Gavin—I thought you did too—I suppose you've quarrelled,' he charged aggressively.

'Don't be silly, Oliver,' she answered crossly. 'You can't always have your own way. You'd like to spend Christmas with Grandma and Grandpa, surely?'

'No—I wouldn't—oh—I wish Daddy was here,' and

Oliver buried his head on the back seat of the car and cried mournfully.

Adele got him straight to bed. He was over-tired after the party, and would feel differently tomorrow she hoped.

At the sight of the suitcase next day Oliver did brighten up, and gathered up a few of his personal things he insisted on taking, but every time he heard a car go along the road outside he raced to the window and on one occasion came back to Adele enthusiastically.

'As long as Uncle Gavin comes before the taxi, we're all packed and ready to go with him, aren't we, Mummy—and you'd *rather* go with Uncle Gavin, wouldn't you?' He bent down and peered up into Adele's face.

Oh, how did you make a four year old understand?

'Darling—Gavin isn't coming here—he wants to be with his mother and Vivien.'

'But he wanted us to go too—he said so, that day he took me to the swing-park.'

'Then he had no right because *I* want to see *my* mummy,' Adele replied flatly.

After that Oliver didn't go to look out of the window again. He became rather subdued as if he had a great problem on his mind.

They were packed and ready—ready to go to the airport to take their chances.

'We might have to wait up all night, darling,' she explained to Oliver, 'so it's best that you have a nap now, then we'll have a cup of tea before we leave. It's such a nuisance we couldn't book, but if we're there we shall be first in the queue if they get a cancellation.'

Oliver went to sleep almost at once. Adele knew she should have told someone where she was going but what could it matter?—everyone had so much to do in preparation for Christmas that it was unlikely anyone would even miss her.

If they did get to Canada and decided to stay on for a while then she would write to Gavin and Mrs Dawkins. Meanwhile there was always the chance that Vivien would return to Beecroft immediately after the holday. Matthew would be needed at the hospital for one thing. Adele decided to leave a note, then she remembered that Vivien had said she would telephone on Christmas morning.

That was still two whole days away. She hoped they would get on a flight—they had to—she couldn't bear Beecroft to be so lifeless as it seemed now.

Carrying the cases down to the hall she saw the telephone answering machine which Bernie had needed for his work standing idle on the shelf beneath the telephone. Now that was a clever idea she congratulated herself and in a few minutes she had recorded this message:

'Adele Kinsey regrets that she is not at home, but wishes the caller a happy Christmas. She and Oliver have gone to Canada for a much needed holiday.'

It sounded so horribly formal, so impersonal, and the croaking of her voice on the final words sent her into a deluge of tears.

CHAPTER ELEVEN

Snow was falling heavily by the time the taxi reached the airport which looked festive, and helped Oliver to forget that Uncle Gavin had let him down badly. There were people everywhere, and Adele soon learned that most flights had been delayed if not cancelled, but she stood her ground, despite being advised to go back home. Somehow she meant to get to Canada. It was imperative. There were too many memories at Beecroft. Memories of happy Christmases when Bernie was alive and well. Not such happy memories of Bernie's last Christmas when he had felt so ill and yet put such a brave face on things for Adele and Oliver's sakes. Memories now came flooding back to taunt Adele. Bernie's death, her grief, the will to survive for Oliver. Matthew and his devotion to her through the dark empty days when just breathing seemed needless effort, and then Gavin. Arrogant and rude she had thought him at first with no consideration for her four year old son. How wrong she had been. How quickly he had shown her how much he cared for Oliver.

Adele glanced down at Oliver sitting beside her on the leather seat, wide-eyed and curious as to all that was going on around him, clutching tightly to a small attaché case in which he carried his prize toy cars. My poor darling, she thought, what am I doing to you? Her eyes filled with tears; if he only knew how much she needed Gavin too, but he was far away at Cedar Grove, entering into the spirit of Christmas with the others, unaware of their despondency.

The time passed slowly even though there was so much to watch. She heard some French people talking and remembered Jacques. So handsome but so smooth. Arrogant and masterful but with only one thought behind it all, to woo his victim towards the nearest bed. Adele's tears changed to

laughter. It was easy to see the amusing side of Jacques now
that it was all over. He thought himself quite irresistible;
she had at least succeeded in hurting his pride. He would
have reached Paris by now, probably enjoying himself with
his side of the family, and she wondered how he would
explain those deep scratches on his face. Had he told Gavin
how he came by them? She was back to Gavin again. She
tried not to think about him but concentrated on people
arriving, coming in with thick snow across their shoulders,
stamping it from their shoes and boots, which in the warmth
of the airport lounge quickly turned to muddy water.

It seemed as if she watched every minute tick by, only
occasionally missing one when she opened chocolate for
Oliver, and towards late evening she went to the cafeteria
and bought coffee, and milk for Oliver, and they enjoyed
the cheese rolls she had packed among other items of food
in preparation of their long wait.

'I think we'd better go to the ladies, Oliver,' she said,
'then you can settle down to sleep while I listen for any
cancellations.'

Adele asked a nearby family to keep their eye on her
suitcases. She attended first to Oliver, wiping his face and
hands with a tissue. She left him sitting on a stool at the
mirror while she went to the toilet.

She listened as an announcement came over the loud-
speaker. It was her name being called! What did they say,
she wondered, not able to catch every word. One thing was
certain, it meant a seat on a plane bound for Canada, and
she hurried, glad that her prayers had been answered so
quickly.

She began walking towards a wash-basin at the same time
looking towards Oliver—to where she had left him—to
where he should have been. He was gone! But only back to
where they'd left their cases, she consoled, and dried her
hands quickly.

There was no sign of Oliver.

'Have you seen my little boy? she asked anxiously of the
people guarding her luggage, and when they said they
hadn't she began to run panic-stricken to the nearest desk.

'You called my name, Kinsey, but my little boy has run off—have you found us seats on a plane?'

Adele felt a tug at her hip-length sheepskin coat.

'We won't need the tickets now, Mummy. Uncle Gavin has come for us.'

Adele turned, relieved at the sound of Oliver's voice, shocked at the sight of him standing there casually holding Gavin's hand.

'You naughty boy, Oliver, you shouldn't have gone off like that,' she reprimanded.

Gavin was speaking to the assistant behind the desk. 'You can cancel that request for tickets to Canada,' he told the girl.

She smiled admiringly at him. 'Just as well, sir, it looks as if most planes will be grounded for the next forty-eight hours.'

Gavin led Adele into a passageway.

'What do you mean by barging in here—?' she began.

'What do you mean, you stupid girl, by telling the world you had gone to Canada?'

'I thought Viv would wonder where I was,' she said meekly.

'I'm glad you did that in time for me to catch you, but supposing someone other than me had telephoned and you had got to Canada—you could have come home to find your home stripped of everything.'

'I . . . I didn't think,' she stammered.

'Do you ever stop to think, fair damsel? Did you really think I would let you spend Christmas alone?'

'How did I know what to think? How do I know what *you're* thinking?' she asked pointedly. 'One moment you're so charming, so persuasive, the next I'm merely one of your staff.'

'Darling, I was so shaken when you told me that you loved me.' He held her arms firmly forcing her to look into his haunting green eyes. 'I was afraid to believe you. I cursed myself for going too fast, for loving you too impetuously. You needed time, Lassie said, and I didn't mean to rush you during that weekend. I know so well all that you've been going through—the hellish void—the struggle to go on—I wanted to help you and Oliver because I understood.'

'But you suddenly stopped caring,' she cried in anguish.

'No, fair damsel, I never stopped caring for one moment. My love for you grew each time I saw you, but I had to square things with Matthew.'

'I'm fond of Matthew, he's been so good to me.'

'And he would have married you,' Gavin assured her.

'If Viv hadn't come into his life—he got love and pity all mixed up where I was concerned. He and Viv are so right for each other, but at first I thought it was you and Viv.'

'Adele, my darling, such needless torment. Viv and I are very close. Probably closer than blood brother and sister, but nothing more than that. Oh, I love you so very much.'

'But I make you angry—you looked at me with such contempt on the night of the party.'

'I should think so too,' he said, suddenly serious. 'Accepting lifts from comparative strangers.'

Adele looked down at her fingers toying with her sheepskin mittens. 'I . . . I hoped you'd offer, but you weren't quick enough, and you didn't even ask me to dance.'

'You seemed to be managing without me—Matthew and Jacques—you looked all set to seduce one of them but I wasn't certain which one.'

'Then you should have been,' she said confidently. 'Only you, Gavin—only you.' Her lips trembled.

He held her close to him unaware of people passing by, glancing their way curiously.

'Are you sure, my darling? If you only knew the battle I've had with my conscience this past month or so. I couldn't trust myself to dance with you at the party. I thought you were being provocative to pay me back for the shocking way I treated you at Cedar Grove. Darling, no way shall I ever measure up to Bernie's standards. It's no good looking for his qualities in me, but I do want you so much.'

'And I you,' she vowed. 'I know you'll be good to Oliver

as well as me. My first marriage was a successful one, not perfect though, Gavin. We had our fights and disagreements just like everyone else, but when you've lost someone so dear, so close, you tend only to remember the good times.'

'We'll have good times too, fair damsel, especially this Christmas. I came back to spend it with you and Oliver if you'll have me.'

'But Lassie and the others?' Adele queried.

'I went out to Cedar Grove to talk things out with Lassie after the party—or rather after I had given my philandering cousin a black eye.'

'You didn't!' Adele exploded.

Gavin laughed. 'Jacques is—mm—more or less harmless—useless with his fists, and he came back to my flat boasting of his conquest with the beautiful widow. When I saw the scratches I guessed that you had protected yourself admirably, but seeing that you're my responsibility I decided a black eye was as good a present as any to match the scored face.'

'Poor Jacques—you shouldn't have,' Adele said sympathetically.

'Well, I like that! Is that all the thanks I get for protecting my property?'

'But I'm not your property.'

'Adele—it's three years ago exactly that Anita died. On the night of the party you reminded me so much of her, slim, vivacious—yes, you were provoking Jacques and Matthew you know, and I had to go away and—and—think—grieve a little too perhaps. I went to my mother because I needed some reassurance—just as you were running away to your mother today.' He bent to kiss her forcibly. 'I'm glad I caught you—Lassie does understand—we'll have our Christmas together at Beecroft, then go to Cedar Grove for New Year.'

'Oh, Gavin, that will be wonderful,' Adele said, tears of happiness brimming over.

They felt a head butting its way between them.

'Come on, Mum, can't we go home now?' Oliver begged

and as they looked down affectionately at him he asked, 'Have you chosen him to be my Dad?'

A contented Oliver slept soundly on Christmas Eve after a busy day of making snowmen, toboganning in the park, lunch at The Golden Eagle and late night shopping, a special sack hanging on the door handle of his bedroom.

Downstairs Adele stood on a chair to tie the last of the gifts on the top of the tree.

'Funny,' she said, 'I still bought presents for a man, it didn't seem right without them.'

Gavin went to her and held out his arms. 'Come down, fair damsel, you haven't given me my Christmas gift yet.'

It's not time for present giving until after church tomorrow morning,' she said falling into his embrace.

'It's time for this one now—tell me again that you love me—tell me again and again,' he decreed.

And she did.